The Best and the Brightest

The VW turned into the Redwood parking lot, which was still almost empty. "Ah, yes," Peter commented. "Micki Greene's land of opportunity for the next four years. Don't worry. You'll be fantastic."

"Really?" She laughed and grabbed his hand.

"Really. My sister is going to be the best freshman Redwood has ever seen. The best and the brightest."

"You sound like Mom and Dad."

"DO IT, MICK!" Peter yelled, giving her a gentle push toward the door. Then the VW door closed; he waved and chugged off.

"Yeah, do it," Micki said to herself as she took another deep breath. "Do it," she said again in a slightly smaller voice.

CLASS of '89

by Linda A. Cooney

Freshman
Sophomore
Junior
Senior

CLASS of '89

FRESHMAN

Linda A. Cooney

SCHOLASTIC INC.
New York Toronto London Auckland Sydney

ISBN 0-590-41674-X

12 11 10 9 8 7 6 5 4 3 2 1   8 9/8 0 1 2 3/9

Printed in the U.S.A.   01

First Scholastic printing, June 1988

FRESHMAN

CHAPTER
1

Micki Greene wanted to be the first one at Redwood High that morning. She didn't care if she was over an hour early and had to wait for everyone else. She had to be the first one there. She *would* be the first.

"Peter, are we there yet?"

"No! And if you tell me you're carsick, I'm pulling over and making you walk."

Micki grinned and sat back in the seat. The little VW was noisy and cramped, and the dashboard and glovebox reminded her of a toy car. But for the moment she couldn't tease her big brother about the rumbling and the rattling. There were too many other things bouncing around her crazy brain.

"See that?" Peter said, pointing out his window to a big black Chevy in the other lane.

"What?" Micki was craning so hard she just

about had her nose up to the window. Her breath was starting to make streaks.

"That's a senior," Peter announced. "Martin Timmarian. His brother is in my dorm. You're not going out with him."

"Why?"

"You're much too smart for him. Besides, he wouldn't be above taking advantage of a fresh — "

"PETER!"

Peter was laughing, and even though Micki was tired of his teasing her about being a first-day freshman, she started laughing, too.

Actually it felt pretty good to laugh, because everything else felt so nutty. Oh, sure, the landscape whirring by looked the same. The grassy slopes that stretched toward calm green mountains were the same ones that Micki had seen a million times before. But those were just the ranches and the vineyards. If you looked at what was *inside* the Volkswagen — and more specifically at Michelle Madelyn Greene — then it was something else entirely.

Micki gripped her new notebook, her thesaurus, her calculator, her computer literacy manual, and her dictionary. Her insides felt like a Pepto Bismol commercial. Her outsides — preened over, worried about, and fussed with until the last hair on her head seemed like it had been arranged a thousand times — were just as out of control. Micki knew it was time to drop the conservative look she had fostered at Portola Middle School, but she wasn't ready for loud colors and glittery jewelry — yet. Maybe someday she'd make as big a statement with her clothes as she did with her personality.

Peter was the conservative type, too. Tweed jackets, close-cropped hair, lime aftershave. He caught Micki staring at him and reached across to poke her. "You look great." He smiled. "Very Micki."

"Thanks."

"I never would have looked so cool when I was a freshman."

"Which was a hundred years ago."

"Only fifty."

Micki poked him back. "Thanks for driving me, too," she said, watching the downtown traffic as they passed the fire station and the mall and the grizzly bear statue in front of Portola Park. Two empty yellow buses chugged past them, heading in the other direction. They disappeared as soon as they turned toward the mountains. "Mom said she'd take me, but that stockbroker's thing came up. And Dad had to meet that mayor guy for breakfast. The bus would have picked me up so late."

"The bus ride would have been gross anyway," Peter replied. "I remember. The seats were stickier than the floor of the Movieplex. Everybody used to put their gum all over the place."

"And you're always telling me how your friends were so mature."

"My friends!" Peter wailed, as if on cue. "MY FRIENDS! My friends were mature compared to all of yours. Does Doug still make jokes all the time and play that saxophone?"

"Doug is talented," Micki proudly protested.

"And Bets," Peter said, referring to Micki's other best friend, Betsy Frank. "The only subject she can discuss clearly is her ranch and her animals. Maybe she should go back to the 4H club."

"Bets is loyal and sweet."

"And what about the rest of them?"

"Peter. My friends are unique."

"I'll say."

"Special."

"Okay. All ten thousand of them."

"Original."

"Enough! I just mean, if you collect a few more of them, I won't be able to phone home anymore."

They both started laughing again, and Micki had to lean out of the way when Peter tried to tickle her.

"There it is," Peter warned as the light changed, and they turned onto Redwood Avenue.

"*OHHHH*," Micki gasped. She could see the campus. It was only a year old and very modern. There were clumps of square, dark-wood classrooms and grass so green it looked dyed. A flag waved at the main entrance, and there was a banner that read WELCOME GRIZZLIES in bold red and blue. Redwood looked five times the size of Portola, where Micki and most of the incoming freshmen had gone to middle school.

The VW turned into the Redwood parking lot, which was still almost empty. "Ah, yes," Peter commented. "Micki Greene's land of opportunity for the next four years."

"Do you think so?"

"Why not? High school is great."

For Peter, high school had been great. He'd

been a Merit scholar. Track star. Homecoming king.

Micki knew that even though she was different from Peter, the same caliber of accomplishment was expected of her. "I think it will be great."

He pulled over by the flagpole and shot her an affectionate smile. "Are you prepared?"

She hugged her books. "Definitely."

"Think you'll survive?"

Micki took several deep breaths — one of the relaxing exercises her mother was always practicing. "Absolutely."

Peter patted her hair. "Don't worry. You'll be fantastic."

"Really?"

"Really. My sister is going to be the best freshman Redwood has ever seen. The best and the brightest."

"You sound like Mom and Dad."

"DO IT, MICK!" Peter yelled, giving her a gentle push toward the door. Then the VW door closed; he waved and chugged off.

"Yeah, do it," Micki said to herself as she took another deep breath. "Do it," she said again in a slightly smaller voice.

"You shouldn't find it too hard to make friends," Mr. Kane told Laurel Griffith. "Most of the incoming freshmen already know one another. They came from Portola Middle School. But you're all freshmen together. So even though you just moved to Redwood Hills, you should do fine."

Laurel put her sketch pad on the attendance

office counter and looked from Mr. Kane, the freshman adviser, back to her dad. There was still nearly an hour before the first day started. In fact it was so early that, besides a few secretaries and Principal Tomasino, the three of them were the only ones there. "As long as I can take a good art class," she told Mr. Kane, "I'll be happy."

Her father put his arm around her. They stood in a straight line surrounded by metal desks, stacks of papers, and walls covered with Grizzly spirit posters and graphs. It wasn't the kind of place a person would normally get excited about, but Laurel found herself taking in the light, the muted colors, and sharp lines as if she were going to draw them.

"Will getting Laurel into advanced art be a problem?" her father asked in his best I-used-to-be-a-teacher-too voice.

Mr. Kane shuffled through a stack of schedule cards, plucked one out, and read it over. "Let's see. It says here that your dad sent some of your cartoons to Mrs. Foley and she okayed you for the advanced class even though you're a freshman. If it's okay with her, it's okay with me."

"Great!" Laurel exclaimed.

She slid her wire-rimmed glasses up like a hair band, pushing her long corn-silk hair away from her face. Moving to Redwood Hills was going to work out, she told herself. Looking into her father's eyes, which were as green as hers, she knew that he was thinking the same thing.

Mr. Kane filled out more papers and cards. The minute hand on the overhead wall clock thunked. Suddenly Mr. Kane stopped writing and looked up at Laurel with a concerned expression. "Laurel, are you sure you really want to be with older kids? That's a pretty serious class, Mrs. Foley's advanced art. It might be better to wait, take every opportunity to get to know kids in your own class first."

Laurel's dad frowned and faced Laurel. "What do you think? Maybe he's right, honey. Maybe you should do whatever you can to get to know other freshmen."

Laurel reached for her sketch pad and stowed it inside the wicker book basket. "I'm not worried about getting to know people," she told them both. "It's not that important to me."

Both men waited for the other to say something. When neither did, Mr. Kane went back to the schedule cards. "Okay. Did your wife sign these, Mr. Griffith?"

Laurel's dad cleared his throat. "It's just me. My wife and I are recently divorced. Just me and Laurel."

"I see. No problem." Mr. Kane scribbled for another minute, then spread the papers out for Laurel. "Here you go. There's a map on top. We're starting today with a freshman orientation in the auditorium. Classes will begin late, just for today."

"Okay."

Laurel's dad checked his watch. "Will you be okay on your own now, honey?" He glanced back at Mr. Kane and told him, "I have to be in class, too. I'm going back to school over at the university."

Mr. Kane nodded and kept writing.

"Go ahead." Laurel reached up and hugged her dad good-bye. He clutched her tightly in return. She wasn't embarrassed. "Dad, I'll be okay," she told him.

"I know. I'll pick you up at three." He smiled, backed toward the teachers' mailboxes, and headed for the door. He waved as he jogged away until he passed the last window and disappeared.

When her dad was gone, Mr. Kane stacked Laurel's cards and papers and handed them to her. "Well, you really are on your own now, Laurel."

"Yes." On my own, Laurel thought. At last. She hugged her basket to her lacy dress and felt like leaping. On her own. That was just the way she wanted it to be.

Page Hain was with her sister, so she didn't have to worry.

Not about her clothes, not about her hair. Not about her freshman classes or her teachers or where she was going to eat lunch. Since the age of ten all she'd been told was that her looks were perfect. She'd gotten good grades at Oakwood Private, and her sister Whitney, a sophomore, had assured her she was going to take care of everything at Redwood, from lunchtime to dating.

The only thing Page was worried about was actually getting to Redwood on time. "Whitney," she told her sister, who dawdled at the entry hall mirror adjusting her makeup. "Do we have to wait for Natalie to drive us?"

Whitney rolled her gray eyes and sighed. "Yes, Page."

Page and Whitney were being driven to school by Whitney's friend Natalie Bonwit, who had also gone to Oakwood Private and drove a new red BMW. Whitney swore up and down that Natalie's Beamer was the only way to make an entrance on the first day at Redwood. Page figured that that was probably true, but she also worried that the BMW would have to drive about eight hundred miles an hour in order to make it there with the rest of her classmates. Whitney didn't care about that, but then Whitney wasn't a freshman.

"It's okay," Whitney soothed, fluffing her dark hair and placing her cheerleading charm just so around her creamy white neck. "Cool out, Page. I'm telling you, if you just relax and leave things to me, this will be the beginning of the best four years of your life. Besides, the first hour is just that freshman orientation. You don't care about that."

"I don't?"

"I'll tell you everything."

"But — "

"Page, just listen to me. I know."

Page wasn't sure how her sister could know, since she was only in the second year of high school herself. But Whitney seemed to know about a lot of things. And their oldest sister Julianne said the same thing, which all pointed to the fact that it was *Page* who didn't know.

"Besides," Whitney smirked, "how else did you plan to get to school? Take the bus? Ride a skateboard?" She chuckled and patted powder over her perfect, pale skin.

It was true. Their family's huge vineyard was all the way on the other side of Capitola Mountain. Walking would take forever, and Whitney said anyone who took the bus was less than hopeless.

"Let's at least wait outside," Page urged as Whitney continued to stare at herself in the mirror.

"Page, can't you ever just relax?"

No, Whitney, I can't relax, Page thought. Not with you breathing down my neck. And not dressed in this ridiculous outfit you're making me wear. Earlier that morning Whitney had told Page to change out of the baggy jeans and soft white shirt Page had chosen for her first day of high school. "No way," Whitney had said. "No little sister of mine is going to be pegged as a slob. Here, wear this," she ordered, pulling a wool skirt out of Page's closet. "Get it together, Page."

Page sighed. Finally she nudged her sister out the front door where they waited on the bench that sat next to the long Hain driveway. The acres of grapevines stretched out to one side, and the sparkly sun made Page wish that summer wasn't over.

"You are so lucky to have me," Whitney told her as she stretched her arms over her head. "You can start hanging out with the sophomores right away. That way you won't have to worry about being pegged with anyone creepy."

"I won't?"

"You can pass the lowlife stuff right by. Just stay by me and act like a grown-up."

Page couldn't argue. Whitney had gone over

this with her too many times already. Stick with her, and Page would have it made. It all gave Page a funny feeling, but then again everything that Whitney said seemed to make sense. She closed her eyes to pray that Whitney was right, and that Natalie Bonwit would gun that BMW and somehow get her to school on time.

The morning cleared, the dew evaporated. Birds looked for worms under the sprinkling system that covered the high school's emerald-green lawns. The parking lot filled with cars. Old cars, new cars . . . Natalie's BMW. Some kids got out of their cars right away. Others lingered as though they'd already made up their minds that most of this new high school year was going to be spent in the parking lot anyway.

There were reunions everywhere. Excited, noisy, show-offy reunions. Schedules were compared, teachers, classes, lunch periods. New clothes were noted. Some were complimented, some not, but almost everything was taken in. In fact, very little was missed in that hour before the first day of school at Redwood.

But there was one student who hadn't got that far and wasn't sure that it really mattered.

Jed Walker was late. Very late, especially since he still had so far to go. His long dark hair fell over the collar of his shirt. His blue eyes were surveying the relentless rush of cars that roared down Corona Boulevard and into town. His thumb was out, but he didn't waste much time on it because he knew his chances of getting a ride were remote. So mostly he walked, with his Levi's jacket wrapped around himself to keep out the wind that was kicked up by the cars.

Jed was a freshman, too. He'd gone to Portola, although most of the people in his class wouldn't recognize his name. Jed was used to that, and there wasn't much he could do to change it. He didn't care what they thought anyway. He preferred to do things his own way.

He stuck his thumb out again. Cars sped by. That was okay, too. He'd get there when he got there. He'd go to the office and tell them freshman orientations just weren't his style. And if they had trouble with it . . . well, that was the breaks. Maybe it was high school, but in a way he'd been through this before. He knew what it was like. He could deal with it.

As far as Jed was concerned, it was just another day.

CHAPTER 2

"Yo, Mick!"

Micki was still waiting in the parking lot where Peter had left her. Waiting, waiting, waiting. It was almost time for freshman orientation to start, and finally Doug and Betsy were jogging over from the street. "Where have you two been?" Micki cried, rushing to meet them. "I was starting to get worried."

"Are we late?" My dad's truck broke down way out on the ranch. And Doug's dad . . . boy, does he drive slow." Bets looked around. "Where is everybody?"

"Carlos and Paul went ahead. The rest are late, too. Our freshman orientation starts in fifteen minutes," Micki worried.

"It's just an orientation. And fifteen minutes is a very long time." Doug leaned over to mess up Micki's hair. "See you've got your back-to-school outfit on. *Très* impressive."

Micki unbuttoned her jacket and twirled around. Doug did a little dance. "You bozo," she laughed. She was so glad to see both of them.

"Me?" Doug was tall, with bright blue eyes that made people laugh without knowing why. He believed in wearing clothes that said something. For day one he'd chosen jeans and green tennis shoes — which was nothing notable — but the T-shirt he had on read PORTOLA MIDDLE SCHOOL RUBE GOLDBERG TOOTHPASTE CHAMPS. And then there was his distinctive haircut, short in front with that skinny blonde ponytail crawling down his neck. Doug called it his "rat tail."

"Mick, you look very Class of '89." Doug laughed.

"You, too."

If Doug and Micki were noticeable from about a hundred yards away, Bets was just the opposite. Her wheat-blonde hair was brushed into a neat pageboy. And her clothes were essential, even-tempered, farm-girl Bets — plaid shirt tucked into brown cords. Even her cowboy boots looked soft and worn and friendly. "You really look pretty," she assured Micki.

Micki didn't like to worry about whether or not she looked pretty. "I'm nervous."

"Don't be nervous," said Bets. Remembering something, she lifted a hand to her freckled face. "Oh. We, um, shouldn't have signed up for Dunbrick for science. Paul O'Conner said he gives homework the first day."

"Uh-oh," Doug and Micki said at the same time.

14

The three of them had different ideas about homework. Micki got hers done way ahead of time; Doug crammed the night before things were due; and Bets inevitably handed things in late. Even their notebooks reflected three different approaches. Micki's contained dividers and calendars and clear zippered sacks. Doug's was covered with as many decals as his saxophone case. Bets's notebook was empty except for a plastic-wrapped packet of paper.

"We'll just stick together," Micki said. "We'll help each other like we always have."

Doug snuck in behind Bets and rested his chin on her shoulder. "Why worry about classes? It's only the next four years we're looking at. I mean if you think of it like a jail sentence, then it's not so bad."

Bets knocked Doug in the stomach with her elbow. "Um, thanks," she said.

"Uh, you're welcome," he replied.

Micki groaned. "Great, Doug. My brother says high school's an opportunity; you say it's a jail sentence. Why is it that neither of you make me feel any calmer?"

Suddenly feeling more sober, they huddled near the flagpole on anxious lookout for the rest of their friends. The September air was as clear as a raindrop, and they could almost smell the grapevines strung up in even rows along the slopes. Meanwhile the year-old school looked like an advertisement for Northern California, with fat trees and tennis courts and pairs of tanned upperclassmen strolling by.

"You know . . ." Bets faltered. She often faltered in the middle of sentences. "I think, um, even I'm kind of nervous."

"Even you?" Doug commented. "Amazing."

"It's okay," Micki assured them, still searching the lot, the street, the bus stop. "We'll survive."

"We have to," Doug laughed. "We've trained for it."

They all laughed. Micki *had* trained them for it. Not just Doug and Bets, but all their friends from Portola. All ten thousand, as Peter would say. Micki had counseled them over the summer. She'd made computer printouts of their schedules on her Apple at home. She'd quizzed Peter on their teachers. Finally she'd led the whole clothes-shopping ritual, which had gone hand in hand with discussions about how the one unique eighth grade class to graduate from Portola would fare as high school freshmen. And here it was about to start, and she felt as panicked as anyone.

Bets sensed Micki's panic right away. As usual, her intuition was in fine form. "What, Micki?" Bets asked. "What are you worried about?"

Doug leaned in, too. "Yeah, Mick, what gives?"

Micki wasn't sure how to explain it to them. She just had such high hopes for herself, Bets, Doug . . . for all of their friends from Portola. In middle school they'd been known as the wacky class, the class that rarely did what they were told, and yet always did something outstanding. Teachers either adored them, or begged never to have them in class again. They'd finally earned some real respect when they placed in the Northern

16

California Rube Goldberg contest last year by creating an elaborate machine that performed the simple function of squirting toothpaste on a toothbrush. It consisted of a shoe kicking a rock . . . that knocked over a stack of cards . . . which pushed a marble down a ramp . . . which flicked a switch . . . and so forth until the toothpaste was squished out. Micki'd organized it with their science teacher, and it had taken a lot of work. Boy, had it taken a lot of work.

But besides the Rube Goldberg machine, the class was also famous for food fights and broken limbs, playing practical jokes on substitutes, and getting kicked out of assemblies. And that was what worried Micki. How would food fights fit in with football games and debate tournaments, SAT's and homecoming, and all the other things Peter and her parents had told her about? This was high school. Micki didn't want to joke her way through things or turn Redwood into a free-for-all. She wanted to succeed, to fly, to really make her mark. For herself and her class.

But she didn't know exactly how to explain this to Doug and Bets, and she didn't want to sound pessimistic on the very first day. "Never mind," she told her friends instead. "It's nothing. We'll be great."

"We will."

"Good."

The peace only lasted a few seconds.

WHOONNNNKKK!

Micki jumped as if she'd felt an electric shock. But even before she was on her feet, she knew what had happened. Doug was up and his saxophone mouthpiece was drooping from the side of his mouth. The sound had set her heart pumping like a steam engine.

"Doug," she laughed.

He continued to play. He also did a weird sort of dance where he tapped his foot and swayed his hips. Bets clapped along.

A group of upperclass girls stopped to stare, and a bulky guy in a letter jacket scowled along with them. Micki simply put her hands on her hips and began dancing, too. She was starting to wonder if they weren't making too much of a scene, when she finally saw two other people from her class. The Dubrosky twins: Jock Mary Beth in spangly pink, and math whiz Alice in conservative navy. It was very Class of '89 for the twins to find Micki and her friends in the middle of a parking lot tango.

Mary Beth yelled, "THERE YOU ARE, MICKI! EVERYBODY'S LOOKING FOR YOU!"

"HURRY UP! WE'RE BUILDING A HUMAN PYRAMID OUTSIDE THE AUDI-TORIUM," blurted Alice.

"YOU HAVE TO SEE IT BEFORE THEY FALL!" they both screamed at the same time. "WE NEED YOU!"

"WE'RE COMING!" Micki yelled back.

The twins ran ahead, and Micki turned back to Doug and Bets. "What a class," she sighed.

"What a planet," said Doug. Bets laughed.

Doug gave one more toot on his saxophone. Then the three of them looked at one another and took off across the parking lot.

*　*　*

Ten minutes later, Bets, Doug, Micki, and most of the rest of their classmates had settled down for orientation. It had taken a while. The human pyramid in the lobby had been a big hit. Unfortunately everybody trying to balance on each other's backs and shoulders had kind of freaked the teachers out. Mr. Kane had yelled at them to stop it before somebody broke a leg. After that, most of the Class of '89 had shuffled into the auditorium.

But not everyone. One girl lingered. Maybe the human pyramid hadn't gone over real big with the teachers, but it had left a big impression on her. So much so that she had hidden in the lobby so she could pull out her sketch pad.

"Amazing," Laurel whispered after the other kids had gone in. She began to sketch with a stick of bright blue chalk.

Laurel's class was amazing. Except that they didn't seem like *her* class. She knew it was too early to make judgments, but she could still tell. They had private looks and inside jokes and pet names. They fell into games as spontaneously as toddlers. It was like being the only stranger at some huge family reunion. Nevertheless, the pyramid had made Laurel think of the circus drawings of Georges Seurat. She had to get it down on paper.

But that meant she was missing orientation. "That's okay," she scrawled in a bubble coming out of the mouth of one her cartoons.

Hidden behind a stack of metal chairs, Laurel was just fine where she was. No one noticed when she hadn't gone in with the others. Her father would have noticed if he had been a teacher here. After the divorce he'd told her she needed friends again, but Laurel knew she only needed her sketch pad, maybe one friend, and some time.

She also knew it would upset him to know that she'd gone back to her old habit of sneaking away and drawing, on the very first day before classes had even started. She used to do it all the time at her old school, and sometimes she got in trouble for it. Nevertheless, it was important. Drawing was like living and breathing for her.

Laurel heard the clack of the lock bar banging into the inside lobby door and looked up to see it being pushed from the other side. A teacher was coming out into the lobby. Laurel closed her sketch pad, put away her chalk, and dusted the blue from her hands. She quickly got up and hurried out the lobby door and down the hall. Her lace-up boots tap-tapped against the linoleum floor, her wire-rimmed glasses slid up and down the bridge of her nose, the straw basket she carried thumped against her hip.

"Made it," she whispered, once she was outside the lobby. She could finish her drawing somewhere else. She looked around and saw the hallways were filled with nonfreshmen catching up on summer. Magazine cutouts were being taped to locker doors. New book covers were being folded, and Laurel could almost smell the ink from all the new textbooks that were being thumbed through.

She wove through the crowd and found the first door that led to the quad. She hurried down past the sculpture garden, then stopped to look out across the tall grass at an old farmhouse on the back edge of school. It was surrounded by a white porch, and the front door was boarded up.

Laurel wondered about the old house. Her dad said it was the only remnant of when the year-old campus used to be a cattle ranch. But it reminded Laurel of her old hiding places, the ones she went to after her mom left. Laurel had to decide not to leave with her, and after that she found herself searching for places where she could be alone. There had been plenty at her old school, but she didn't know yet about Redwood. The old farmhouse looked tempting.

Laurel had taken a few steps into the tall grass toward the house when a trio of upperclass girls jangling their car keys started heading in the same direction. Laurel changed course, backed away from the farmhouse, and toward the side field. She went fast and finally reached an area that seemed separate from the rest of the school. Instead of square wood-sided classrooms, these were two long metal buildings, like Quonset huts or small indoor tennis courts. She wondered if this might finally be the place where she could sit privately and draw.

She trotted up three steps, then squinted at the door. INDUSTRIAL ARTS read a small white sign. The air was still summery warm and the light was fine for drawing. All in all, it felt pretty safe. Laurel thought of the wildflowers she sometimes saved to draw; she'd store them between sheets of waxed paper. She felt almost as safe as those petals now, as set aside and wrapped up.

With her back against the shop door, Laurel sat cross-legged and pulled her sketch pad out of her book basket. She was searching through her chalk box, when suddenly the door behind her burst open, whacking her in the back, and almost thrusting her halfway down the walk.

"Ow!" she cried, scrambling to her feet.

"What are you doing here?" demanded a boy standing in the doorway. He had inky blue eyes and dark hair that flopped over his forehead. He wore old jeans and a torn denim jacket over a plain white T-shirt. The toe of one of his tennis shoes was mended with wide silver tape.

"Sitting. What does it look like?"

"Well, you shouldn't sit there. How was I supposed to know you were there?"

"I don't know, but you could at least say 'I'm sorry'! You almost knocked my brains out."

"Well, I just got here this second. I was late." They glared at one another. Finally he shrugged. "Sorry."

Laurel saw that her basket had been knocked over and her sketch pad and books were scattered across the walkway. There were drawings of her old school and her best friend in San Jose. Most private of all, there were sheets and sheets of bold blue stars. They stood for her mom who had left so quickly, who had never forgiven Laurel after Laurel chose her father.

The boy glanced over the drawings; then his gaze came back to her. "Are you hurt or anything?" he finally asked.

"No."

"Do you need something?"

Laurel was hastily picking up her things. "No, I don't." She remembered that she wasn't supposed to be out there, and looked around for teachers.

The boy looked around, too. He hunched his shoulders to raise his jacket collar higher around his neck. His face was flushed, as if he'd walked a long way very quickly, and there was a trickle of sweat above his lip. "So what are you doing here?"

"I told you. I was sitting. Drawing. I like to draw and paint. Is that okay?"

"Don't ask me. I just started here."

"Oh. You're a freshman, too."

He nodded.

"What's your name?"

"Jed. Jed Walker. How come you're not at that orientation thing?"

Laurel looked around again. Finally she took her glasses off and cleaned them on her dress. "I just moved here. I had a special orientation for new kids last week." She slipped her glasses back on to see if he believed her lie. He didn't seem to question her. "What about you?"

"I got here too late. I didn't want to walk in late. Those kids make such a scene out of everything."

"You know everyone?"

He laughed. Then he shifted and pushed his dark hair off his forehead. His hands were graceful and slender, hands that Laurel couldn't help but notice would be good to draw. "Sort of. I went to Portola."

"It seems like such a tight crowd."

"That's the understatement of the century." He looked out past her again, checking to see if anyone was coming.

"I guess it will just take time to get to know people. That's what my dad says."

"Oh," Jed said, as if he'd just made some great discovery. "You're one of those," Jed decided.

"One of whats?"

"A joiner."

"Me?"

Jed tapped a finger against his forehead and leaned against the doorway with his arms folded over his jacket. Laurel could see past him into the shop. There was a lift like the ones at gas stations, tools hanging on the walls, and lights in metal cages that reminded her of pineapples. "I can tell," he assured her.

"Tell what?"

"You're a joiner. But let me give you a little advice before you go busting your chops to get into that crowd."

"I'm not busting my chops!"

He smiled at her as if he were eons older and doing her some great favor by telling how the world worked. "This is how it is," he said, leaning in and lowering his voice. "Those kids do everything together, and they all think it's so great to be part of their group. They like to peg each other and decide who gets in and who doesn't."

Laurel wasn't sure about pegging people. From what she'd seen of the Class of '89, they just liked each other too much to be interested in someone new. "That isn't what it seemed like to me," she challenged.

24

He turned away with an arrogant lift to his chin. "Make up your own mind. But I'm telling you, the best thing to do is stay totally away from it. From everybody. The only person you can trust is yourself. You remember that."

This boy was making Laurel feel more left out than she had felt sitting alone in the lobby. She believed in being on her own, but she also hoped that she'd find at least one friend at Redwood!

"I'll remember that," she finally answered half-heartedly. She backed down the steps and swung her basket over her shoulder. " 'Bye," she said as she headed back toward campus.

He stood there like a castaway on a desert island. " 'Bye."

"See you around," she called back.

He waved. "I doubt it."

"Fine with me."

Laurel hugged her pad to her chest and walked back toward the auditorium as fast as she could.

CHAPTER 3

Friends were all over the place. So many friends that the Redwood cafeteria seemed as though it were squirming. Friends looking into each other's lunch sacks. Friends trading apples for Twinkies. Friends picking things off each other's trays. But Micki's friends — all ten thousand of them — hadn't made it to the cafeteria yet, and that gave Micki a chance to figure out how the lunchroom worked.

She'd been taking charge of things since after the orientation this morning. First period, Mr. Dunbrick, their science teacher, *had* assigned homework — a chart of the planets, due in two weeks. So as soon as the class was over, Micki had organized a mad scramble. In the end they'd all agreed to create a group project. Paul O'Conner, who was famous for his ability to find materials, had already spotted some Styrofoam blocks in a Redwood Dumpster. That had given

John Pryble the idea of carving the blocks into spheres and hooking them up electrically so they would rotate. Of course, they all got in trouble for being tardy to second period, but how important could a tardy mark be compared to rotating planets?

Micki knew that if she could handle science class, she could certainly handle this lunchroom. Although right now it was nuts: clanging plates, squeaking chairs, and two hundred people gossiping all at once. Micki's task was to maneuver her way through all this upperclass chaos, find a table for her friends, and spot them when they came in. Simple, Micki told herself. Do it.

A tall senior almost stepped on her toe, and Micki nearly ran into another girl who was holding her lunch tray up so high it looked as if she were avoiding a flood. Finally she spotted a big, round table, completely free, right in the middle of the caf. Micki zoomed over to it and spread her lunch and books and pencil sharpeners and folders around as if they were favors at a birthday party. Now all she could do was wait for the guests. But she didn't have to wait for very long. Doug and Bets were squeezing their way through the front entrance.

"OVER HERE. DOUG!!! BETTSSSS! OVER HERE!"

Micki waved like mad. They saw her stuff spread out over the table and flocked to it. As Doug and Bets made their way over, Micki gestured again and more of the Portola gang appeared. There was Paul O'Conner, the salvage man, in his overalls and baseball cap. The

Dubrosky twins with super-tanned Cindy White. Cute Carlos Oneda, who could talk anyone into anything. Carlos's best friend, John Pryble, and punked-out Sarah Parker, who'd saved the Rube Goldberg project with her skills as a debugger.

"Hey, Micki," Carlos yelled as he got closer, "you saved this table for us?"

"You got it, Carlos."

Paul plunked down a hunk of Styrofoam while Sarah took off her Walkman and ruffled the skunk-like stripe in her short hair.

Eventually everybody settled into a place. "Well? What do you think?" Micki asked.

The freshmen looked out over the cafeteria as if they weren't sure they were really allowed to be there. They'd all heard horror stories about how hard it was for freshmen to get a decent table. Peter'd told Micki about kids who'd spent their entire first year eating in the hall or at those lonely benches along the wall.

"Boy," Bets complimented, plopping down next to Micki. "This is great."

"Good work, Mick."

"You did it."

"Thanks."

Doug slung a lumpy plastic bread bag on the table. Bets more demurely set out a Thermos and two Tupperware bowls containing homegrown tomatoes and some kind of pudding. Paul opened his lunch box. Cindy uncapped her low-fat cottage cheese. Sarah took out two rolls of sushi. Micki was the only one who'd arrived early enough to buy a cafeteria special.

"So how's it going?" Micki asked in an energetic voice. After first period, their schedules had split them up. Luckily Micki still had third-period English with Doug and fourth-period gym with Bets and the twins. "I want the full report. No censorship allowed."

"Day one is pretty good," Bets volunteered. "Except I spent half of Mrs. Barrie's class writing notes to the people who, you know, weren't in first period with us. Um, to tell them about the planet project. Mrs. Barrie caught me." Everyone nodded sympathetically. If Micki was the protein powder that got the group moving, Bets was the warm glass of milk that made them feel cared for and calmed them down.

Doug, on the other hand, was a shaker of chocolate jimmies. He made everyone laugh. "My day is okay," he told them. "I think I can get into the marching band!" Everyone applauded. "But I almost got thrown out of PE."

"Doug, not again." Carlos winced.

"T-shirts," Doug said briefly. He looked twice at the sandwich before taking his first bite. Doug's mother was almost sixty years old, and his dad was even older, so he sometimes got lunches that were a little old-fashioned. Today he had deviled ham on white bread, cut in four pieces. No crusts.

"I bet I have that same problem," sighed Sarah.

"I just wore my gray T-shirt with the picture of the talking pig on it."

"Doug!" Micki shook her head, and everybody at the table giggled. That was another thing about Doug having such old parents. They didn't seem to catch on that his clothes were offbeat or his jokes or his haircut. Micki's parents were always telling her how she should dress sensibly and tie back her hair. Two of her mom's favorite subjects were "How to make a good first impression" and "The importance of dressing for success."

Micki looked down at her classmates and shrugged. "So that's it? No other news besides PE? Come on. There must be more exciting stuff than that."

She looked around in anticipation. Paul mentioned all the discarded empty boxes outside his computer class, and Sarah told how she'd already helped her Spanish teacher figure out the new intercom system. The twins finished each other's sentences as they described the elaborate decorations they had put up in their lockers. Then they all stopped talking at the same time and dug into their food.

For a while it was just hungry chewing and gulping until Micki suddenly noticed that Bets's fork was at half mast. A wedge of tomato plopped onto the table. Then Doug followed Bets's gaze and he stopped eating, too. A pall fell around the freshman table like a stack of dominoes. Finally Micki put her fork down, wondering what it was that could make an entire table go pale. She looked up and saw two beautiful girls sneering down at their table.

"Hi."

"Oh. Hi."

Two girls were posed right next to Micki, one of whom had just greeted her in a tone that was hoarse and wintery. The other girl stood behind her, looking composed, cool, and quiet.

Micki took one of her deep breaths. When no

one else chimed in, she turned around. "Happy lunch," she told them.

No response. The Class of '89 was as silent as the second girl, although not nearly as composed. Doug still had his crustless sandwich posed next to his mouth, while Bets was dabbing salad dressing off her cuff. Carlos and John held their chins in their hands and gawked at the girls with open mouths.

"You all must be freshmen," the husky-voiced girl finally said, while the other girl stared off across the caf.

They had to be sisters. The one who spoke looked older. She was really decked out in a sweater dress that matched her fluffy dark hair. The younger sister wore a sparkling pink silk shirt and a long wool skirt. Her long hair was simply cut. The one unusual thing about her outfit was a pair of mismatched sparkly earrings — one blue, one white. She looked oddly uncomfortable in what she was wearing, but the effect was stunning. These girls were two of a kind. Both had the same gray eyes; flawless white skin; and fine, elegant bones. Micki patted down her unruly hair and tried to smile.

"I'm Whitney Hain," the older girl said, extending a creamy hand. Three Swatch watches wound their way up her wrist. "This is my sister Page." Page tipped her face in their direction. In that split second Micki realized that she was even more beautiful than her older sister.

Micki introduced herself and her friends. "And we *are* freshmen," she added boldly, even though she knew it was obvious.

"Well, that explains the mistake, and I understand."

"What mistake?"

Whitney reached inside the cowl neck of her dress and pulled out a gold chain, twisting it around her finger and displaying a megaphone charm with a raised red "R." "This is the cheerleaders' table. It was our table all last year. There was no way for you to know."

Some of the Portola gang began gathering their books, and Bets put the lids on her Tupperware containers.

Micki looked around at her friends, surprised at how easily they were giving in. She knew that the Class of '89's zaniness would clash with cheerleaders and older sosh types. But she saw no reason to fold on the first day of school. "I didn't know there were certain tables for certain people," Micki said proudly.

"Like I told you, it's an understandable mistake. There's room on the benches against the wall."

Whitney pointed to the skinny bleacher benches that were on wheels in case they ever needed to turn the cafeteria into a meeting hall. Micki felt a little chill when she took in the sad souls dotted along those side benches. Each of them sat alone — reading . . . scribbling . . . staring intently into space. They looked like they weren't really doing anything, except trying to convince the other kids that they didn't mind sitting solo. Those kids had nothing to do with her and her ten thousand friends.

"Like I said, since you weren't here last year you obviously didn't know," Whitney continued. "It's really important that we have a place to meet and go over our plans for the first football game. It's this Friday. I'm sure you understand."

Whitney's dusky voice wafted on, but Micki had tuned out. Her mind was stuck on one girl at one of those lonely side benches. The girl's corn-silk hair hid half her face and she was scribbling in a sketch pad, staring down through wire-rimmed glasses.

Micki recognized her. She was one of the few freshmen who hadn't gone to Portola or nearby Oakwood Private. She'd just moved here and she was in fourth-period gym, the same class as the twins, Micki, and Bets. She stood next to Micki for roll call because her name was Laura Griffin or something like that. Micki'd wondered why she was so quiet during class, but now Micki found herself wondering about something else.

That girl wasn't the only one in her gym class. Page Hain was in that gym class, too! She had stood on the other side of that Laura Griffin girl; and that meant that gorgeous, cool Page Hain was also a freshman. Instead of joining her class, Page was ganging up with her older sister to work against them. Micki found that shocking. Low. "I didn't see a 'cheerleaders only' sign on the table," she said boldly.

"Excuse me?" Whitney replied.

"A sign. I didn't see a reserved sign. Did you, Dougo?"

"Nope."

"How about you, Sarah?"

Sarah had her Walkman over her ears. The metal band on top cut her skunk stripe in half. "Huh? Oh. No way."

Whitney fumed. "What is that supposed to mean?"

"It means," Micki continued, gaining momentum, "that if this is a cheerleaders-only table, how come your sister, who's a lowly freshman just like we are, gets to sit here? Did she miraculously make the squad this morning? I didn't hear an announcement. You'd think they would have said something over the monitor — freshman makes the cheerleading squad through magic, time travel, astral projection."

Her friends supported her with a few "yeahs," "right, Micki's," and a smattering of applause.

Page reddened and stepped forward. But Whitney pushed her back, slapped down her books to claim her territory, and cut her sister off. "Page went to Oakwood Private — "

"Oh, that explains everything," quipped Cindy.

Whitney's pursed bow mouth was starting to quiver, "And besides that, she's my little sister. I'm sorry, but this is our table. So would you mind clearing your stuff and cleaning up your mess before my friends get here!"

Bets was on her feet. "Let's go, Micki," she urged. "We can sit on the benches or go out in the hall." She backed away from the table, and everyone started collecting their things.

"We don't have to sit in the hall," Micki told them. She looked around for another table, but now the cafeteria was completely jammed.

Bets was tugging her. "Well, this is their table," she reasoned. Nobody else said anything. Doug was telling jokes with Carlos as if this whole thing didn't even matter.

Micki thought for a minute. This was another concern she had about her class. When their peculiar way of doing things worked out they were unstoppable, but when they hit more normal kinds of stumbling blocks they had a tendency to fall apart. Already they were heading for the cafeteria door, laughing at Doug's jokes and not looking back.

Micki finally scooped up her books, too. There was no one left to fight for, and after all, it was only a lunch table. "It's all yours," she told the Hain sisters in a grumpy voice. She left her tray. She wasn't hungry anymore.

Whitney sat down and started gesturing for more upperclass cheerleading types to join her. "Thank you," she answered in an ungrateful voice.

"Oh, any time."

Micki stuck around for one more moment, staring at the back of Page Hain's perfect head. Micki was daring her fellow freshman to look her in the eye, to admit that she was a snob, a traitor to her class. But Page refused to look up from the tabletop.

Micki finally gave up. Shaking her head so hard that her hair brushed against her mouth, she made her way to the door. Bets was waiting for her. Together they found the rest of the gang halfway down the hall, sitting in a big circle as if they were at a meeting for Indian Guides. Micki walked down and stood behind Doug.

"You guys," Micki told them. "I don't think we can block the hallway like this."

Doug was tossing grapes into the air and catching them with his mouth. He tilted his head back, grabbed Bets's boot, and tried to walk his hand up her leg. Bets slapped his hand away.

"We have to find a place of our own for lunch," Sarah was saying.

"Where?" answered the twins at the same time.

"Yeah," echoed Cindy. "Where are we supposed to go?"

"We'll find somewhere," Micki told them. They all looked up at her and smiled. "Don't worry."

She grabbed one of Doug's grapes before he could pop it in his mouth and sat down to join her friends.

CHAPTER
4

All week junior Jason Sandy had been searching for freshmen.

Popular freshmen, unpopular freshmen, good-looking freshmen, ugly-looking freshmen, smart freshmen, dumb freshmen, Jason didn't care. What mattered to him was that they were young, they were impressionable, and there were a lot of them. As far as Jason was concerned, freshmen didn't have a lot of distractions and excuses like older kids, and they had the kind of energy that a yell leader dreamed about. The only problem was that Jason hadn't been able to find them.

On Monday, the very first day of school, he'd spotted a huge group of them as soon as he burst into the cafeteria. But he was late getting to lunch that first day, and by the time he grabbed a sandwich and said hello to everybody, the freshmen were gone. Jason was puzzled.

Tuesday had been just as frustrating. The freshmen hadn't shown up in the lunchroom at all, as far as he could see. He didn't really know any of them, so cruising after school didn't do any good either, because he couldn't recognize faces. He only found a few "loner" kids, who didn't seem to care about their class. He'd tried the main office to see if he could get a list of incoming freshmen from the attendance secretary, but she told him that it wasn't ready yet. Jason had struck out.

But finally on Wednesday, Jason decided to take things in hand. Just moments after the final bell rang, Jason did what had come to be known on campus as his "O.J. Simpson"; his energetic sprint from his last class to his locker, where it seemed he dashed over, under, and around about half of the Redwood student body. Anybody else would have been nailed for sprinting down the hallway, but not Jason. Part of it was that he was head yell leader. Most of it was that he was so energetic it seemed impossible to stop him. He didn't just run — he ran and waved, he ran and slapped shoulders, he ran and patted heads.

In fact it was impossible to slow Jason down unless he really wanted to be slowed down. Everybody knew that, so it was all the more special if the head yell leader took time to stop and talk. That Wednesday, between the dodging and ducking and waving, Jason did stop in the hallway between the art complex and the science wing. He swung his letterman's sweater over his shoulder; anchored his notebooks to his side; and smiled that peppy, famous Jason smile of his.

"Whitney! What's going on?"

Whitney tossed her fluffy hair and smiled right back. "Jason! I'm just going to practice. Where are you going? I thought we were meeting outside the gym."

Jason looked behind him at the side of the gym, which was decorated with a red Redwood grizzly bear. "We are." He rocked on his heels, his spit-shined loafers making clicking sounds against the walk. "I have to do something first. Start without me. I won't be long."

Whitney's pale face wrinkled up.

Jason laughed, snapped one of his suspenders, and then motioned to Page. "Hi, Page."

"Hi," Page answered quietly.

Page stared into a classroom window, and Jason took a moment to admire her. Her face was flawless. Unlike Whitney, who did everything to show her looks off, Page wore her long, dark hair simply. And ever since the second day of school, she'd had on the simple clothes she preferred. But she had the kind of beauty that made it hard not to just stand there speechless and stare.

"Jason," Whitney insisted, drawing his attention back to her. "What are you doing? We only have two days before the first game." She wore three Swatch watches, as usual, and checked all of them. "I don't think we're ready."

Jason tapped Whitney on the tip of her nose. "I know."

"Well, if you know, what could possibly be more important than practice?"

"The freshman spirit rally. I have to find that

39

big crowd of freshmen and pep them up, or they won't even come to the first rally on Friday afternoon. The only freshmen I've been able to talk to so far are the loner kids, the ones that don't hang out with the main crowd. And as you know, they're not the easiest ones to get to spirit rallies."

Whitney didn't look convinced.

"Look, Whitney, if I don't get them to that rally, then they might not come to the game that evening. I don't care how good we are, it's not going to matter if nobody's there to cheer."

"I guess you're right," Whitney finally acknowledged. Even Page managed a tiny nod.

Jason knew he was right. Because if there was anyone who cared about school spirit and having a school he could be proud of, it was Jason Sandy. Sometimes he cared so much he almost exploded with it. And this year, his junior year as head yell leader, he cared more than ever.

And that's why he had to work harder than ever. Last year had started off like gangbusters with a brand-new school and incredibly high hopes. The Class of '88 raised money for the stadium lights by turning the old farmhouse into a great haunted house, and things looked as if they were off to an ideal start. The only problem was the football team. They were terrible. Every time they lost, the spirit went further and further downhill. Jason had been one of the few people to save things. For the homecoming parade he'd come up with the idea of a lawn-chair brigade, kids folding and unfolding lawn chairs with military precision. It was the hit of the year.

He'd gotten kids involved and excited, and the brigade was probably why he'd won yell king.

But this year the football team didn't look any better. And Jason knew that there were upperclassmen looking for any excuse to be apathetic. Jason would do anything to prevent that. He had to. Convincing the Hain girls was part of the program, but Whitney wasn't giving him much help.

"From what I've heard. . . ." Whitney was looking around the hall to see if anyone was in hearing distance besides her little sister. She leaned toward Jason. "Nothing having to do with this freshman class is going to be easy."

Jason looked puzzled for a second. "Is that true, Page?"

Whitney stepped in front of Page before she could answer. "I don't mean Page," she pronounced. "Page went to Oakwood Private, so she's not part of that group. And I'm going to see that it stays that way. But from what I hear of that Portola mob, they're uncontrollable, Jason. Not capable of being organized. Don't waste too much effort on them."

Jason frowned and looked back out across the hall, as if he might spot one of these Portola kids and make a Grizzly convert right there. "Look," Jason said, "we can't give up on anyone. Page, do you know where that big freshman crowd goes after school? Mr. Dunbrick told me something about a bunch of them staying to work on some planet project." Jason laughed before Page could answer. "Actually, Dunbrick was kind of ticked off. I guess he didn't give them permission to do the assignment together."

"See what I mean?" Whitney pointed out.

Jason ignored Whitney and addressed Page. "Do you have any idea where I could find them?"

"I heard some girls in my gym class talk about meeting in the empty art room," Page admitted. "The one they're going to turn into a theater."

Whitney looked at her sister, appalled. "How do you know that?"

"I don't talk to them," Page huffed. "I just overheard."

With that, Jason was moving. Down the hall and yelling back to the girls. "Thanks. Whitney, start practice without me! 'Bye, Page."

Before Whitney could protest, he was out of earshot. He made it to the art rooms in record time, and looked things over. Across the way was a blocky concrete building, the last unfinished bit of their new campus. It had originally been intended as an art studio, but recently it was decided to turn it into a small theater. The funds hadn't been raised yet, so as of now it was still an empty concrete box.

Cautiously Jason went to the doorway to observe. He'd found the Class of '89 all right. The walls and floor were cold, bare concrete, and the air was misty with white dust. But the liveliness of the freshmen made Jason feel as if he were in the tropics.

Nine Styrofoam balls were lined up like planets, and the students were working on making them turn in succession. They were laughing, commenting, debugging, brainstorming. A tall blond boy was providing upbeat mood music on a saxophone, and a girl in cowboy boots was giving away brownies and cartons of milk. Jason, who appreciated attractive girls, watched her. She was rosy-cheeked and carelessly dressed, rangy and doe-eyed in that freshman way that reminded him of a little kid.

Then Jason spotted the girl who seemed to be in charge of things and his interest in this group increased. This girl had thick sandy hair in a shoulder-length tangle, and a curvy figure under too-conservative clothes. She moved almost as quickly as he did and seemed to laugh even more easily. He found himself admiring her, the way he'd admired Page. And yet this girl was the opposite of icy-perfect Page. She wasn't quite as pretty, but she seemed about ten times more fun.

Jason smiled and clapped his hands together, stalling another minute before making his entrance. He liked watching this kind of spirit, and he had to figure out how it would best benefit Redwood. If he could harness their energy, he could send Redwood High to the stars.

"Okay, John, try it again," Micki urged.

Doug took the saxophone out of his mouth and they all stared at Mercury. John, crouched over a homemade motor housed in a shoe box, carefully touched the ends of two wires together. For a moment everyone — Paul, Sarah, the twins, Carlos, Bets, Doug, and freshmen who weren't even in their class — held their breath. They were waiting to see if the first planet would rotate.

It didn't.

"Oh, no."

"Bummer."

"I thought we fixed it."

Doug blew a discouraged note on his saxophone, and Bets moaned. Nobody gave up, though. A moment later they were all scurrying.

"Try oiling the gears."

"Maybe some glue gunked it up."

"I'll check the cord going to Venus."

John tinkered over the motor, but when they tried it again they still came up with nothing. Usually John Pryble could figure out anything electrical, and if he goofed up, Sarah could always debug and redo. But this project had them stumped. Micki wondered if it was the room, or maybe the plaster dust, or the fact that they were in high school now. But it just didn't seem to be working.

Micki'd been wondering about her class ever since that lunchroom scene on Monday. Every day in gym class she watched Page Hain and thought about the difference between her gang and a girl like Page. She'd even found out that Page was not only gorgeous, she was part of the wealthy Hain Winery family. Not that Micki and her friends were dirt poor. Actually her family lived in the newest housing development up on Capitola Mountain. Her mom even drove a new Saab. But there did seem to be a difference.

"Maybe the battery I found is dead," said Paul.

"Try it again and let me look," ordered Sarah.

"Micki," said Carlos, "what do you think?"

They all looked at her. Micki held up the note-book she used to keep track of all their notes and ideas and experiments. "We'll figure it out. We don't give up."

They went back to work while Micki looked through her notes again and tried to see if she could think of an idea. They hadn't given up. That was for sure. This room had become their lunch area, and every day more freshmen joined them to eat there.

Micki was on her way over to join them when she suddenly noticed a new face in her freshman crowd. She stared because she'd noticed him on campus before — he was one of those boys whom every girl noticed. And he definitely wasn't a freshman.

He had dark, curly hair and a dimple dented the center of his chin. He wore suspenders and a letter sweater with so many spirit buttons it looked like a constellation on his chest. He came closer, and she saw that he had the brownest eyes this side of a koala.

"I'm Jason Sandy," he said in a voice vibrant enough for everyone to hear. All the freshmen halted their work and looked over. Yet his eyes were on Micki. "I'm head yell leader."

"I'm Michelle Greene."

Jason smiled and rocked on the balls of his feet. Micki found herself watching him and rocking, too.

"I can see you're all busy, so I don't want to keep you. I just wanted to make sure you all know about the spirit rally this Friday. Right after school, before the first game. You all have to be there because we're going to announce the upcoming social events, and most importantly, we're going to tell you about homecoming." He raised his hands and cheered. "You're Grizzlies now and you have to act like Grizzlies! Right?"

Nobody cheered back. There was a pause while they all looked at Jason and then a few went back to their work. Somebody grumbled something under his breath. Doug played a few scales. Bets brought John another brownie.

Jason's brow creased with concern.

Micki knew what was wrong. Her class had never liked being told who they were and how they were supposed to act. She hated seeing the sad disappointment in Jason's sweet puppy eyes. "I'll remind everyone," she assured Jason.

"Will you?" he asked, turning to her.

Micki nodded. "My class has its own way of doing things. Don't worry."

"You're sure?"

"Leave it to me."

He took a step toward her and smiled. "Okay." Micki watched that dimple sink more deeply into his chin. "I will."

For a moment Micki stood there, staring up at him. Then she felt so warm inside she was almost tipsy, and she realized that Jason had ever so lightly taken her hand. Still watching her, he fished a pen from his pocket. Then he turned her hand over and printed on her palm. Micki watched each letter appear. His writing tickled, but she didn't laugh.

46

"Here's the time of the rally, so you won't forget," he told her. "It's in the aud. You and your class will have to make a float for homecoming. That's the first important thing you have to do for your school."

Micki nodded as if her head were on a string. As much as she tried to look as if she was in control, she felt as if she'd just been shot into orbit. Bets sometimes talked about how she didn't understand boys at all, and Micki often gave her advice, but in reality she made the advice up or lifted it from magazines. She certainly hadn't had much experience herself. None, actually.

Jason finished with a squiggle down her ring finger. "It's important for you to be at this rally. We're going to have a homecoming princess from each class this year, and you don't want to miss out on that."

"Me?" Micki gasped.

"You." He recapped the pen and let go of her hand. "I'll let you all get back to your work, but I'll see you on Friday."

"Okay," she called, watching him run out. He jumped at the exit and tapped the top of the doorway. "See you Friday!"

She stared at the empty door frame and felt a funny kind of victory. After that lunchroom scene on Monday, she'd had this itchy little fear that her class might be lost in this big world called high school. But maybe it was going to be okay.

At just that moment there was a rousing cheer. Micki was still feeling so hazy and light that for a second she thought the cheer was for her and

Jason. But then she turned around and looked at the Styrofoam planets. Mercury was turning — a slow, even spin.

"Fantastic!" Micki cried. She clapped her hands and cheered more loudly than anyone.

CHAPTER 5

"Let's try this one more time," Jason shouted.
"Give me a G."

"G!"

"Good. Give me an R."

Giggles and hand claps. "R."

"Give me an I."

"R."

"Ohhh," Micki sighed.

She couldn't believe it. It was Friday afternoon, the first freshman spirit rally. Jason Sandy was up on the auditorium stage, shouting like a drill sergeant. Whitney Hain and the other cheerleaders were bouncing around like steel marbles, and Micki's class — the Class of '89 — was acting like a bunch of bozos.

If Jason told the freshmen to lean to the left, they leaned to the right. If he told them to stand up, they sat down. When he told them to clap, they whistled, and when he told them to stamp

49

their feet, nobody did a thing. Worst of all, Micki was feeling totally confused.

Since she'd first seen Jason, she'd found herself daydreaming about him in the middle of classes. She'd picture how his hair curled over the tops of his ears, the energetic way he wedged his fingers in his suspenders. She'd written his name on her book cover fifty times — and erased every letter because she'd decided that she was foolish to daydream about a popular junior. She wasn't Page Hain. She wasn't some upperclass cheerleader. She was freshman class dynamo, Micki Greene. That's how she would make her mark. And for this first week, that seemed to be working out.

Now there was this — the entire freshman class acting like a bunch of goof-offs. And to make things worse, Whitney was up there looking like every stupid thing the freshmen did was just what she had expected. The Class of '89 seemed to be playing into her hands.

Micki shifted uneasily in her seat. "This is kind of embarrassing, you know," she commented. "We can't even spell. It's a good thing we're not the Redwood Aardvarks."

Bets giggled. She was sitting next to Micki and Doug. They were playing a game where Bets blew a bubble of pink bubble gum and Doug tried to pop it in her face. Neither one of them seemed overly worried about the way their classmates were behaving.

Micki tried again. "Why do you think our class acts like this sometimes?"

"Hormones," Doug commented.

Micki nodded. "Unhappy childhoods."

"I think this is fun," Bets insisted.

Doug shot over to attack one last bubble, which he smashed all over Bets's face. She slapped his hand and giggled again.

Micki sighed. If Doug and Bets didn't take things seriously, then what hope was there for the rest of the kids? Already Whitney had led the other cheerleaders off the stage in disgust. Jason was at the microphone, explaining in an overly patient voice how important school spirit was, and what a big difference the freshmen were going to make. Micki listened carefully when he brought up freshman princess. There would be a princess from each class, plus a king to represent the seniors. Not that Micki ever thought she was the princess type. Still! . . .

"We'll be playing the Cotter Valley Cavemen for homecoming, so that's the general theme for the floats," Jason was telling them.

He went on about how each class was responsible for a float and that there was some kind of contest the Lions' Club was sponsoring. The Lions had raised money to fix up the old farmhouse on campus, and the class that made the best homecoming float would help decide what the renovated building would be used for in the future.

Doug and Bets finally stopped fooling around and listened. Everyone knew about the old farmhouse, even though it was supposed to be off-limits. Last year the farmhouse had been used as a Halloween Haunted House, which had given the old building a definite mystique.

"We could make it into anything we wanted," Micki grinned.

"Maybe it could be a farmhouse again," Bets speculated.

"I'd prefer a video parlor."

"No, really," Micki insisted. "It would have our class's name on it forever, and it would be whatever we chose. Think about it, Doug. You could make it a room for concerts."

For once Doug looked serious. "Hmmm."

"Or for 4H," she added, even though she knew that Bets had outgrown 4H and was embarrassed by how much she used to like it. Still, Bets smiled. "I know! We could turn it into a place where we can work on projects and where only the Class of '89 can eat lunch!"

"Anyway, as I was saying," Jason reiterated from the front of the auditorium, "the contest is not really the important thing. What really matters is the parade itself. The first game is tonight at eight o'clock. We want to blow that stadium apart."

Jason waved Whitney and her buddies back onstage, but Whitney would only come as far as the side curtain. She posed sullenly with her pompoms on her hips. Jason gestured with increasing frustration, then turned back to the freshmen, embarrassed but trying to appear cool. "SCHOOL SPIRIT IS THE MOST — " he yelled.

"The most what?" Henry Kuy, a kid who sat behind Micki in science class, hooted in a show-me voice.

"What about the farmhouse?" yelled Mary Beth Dubrosky.

"Let's make another haunted house!" sang Alice.

"A haunted house. All right."

"YEAH!!"

"Boo. Wooooo."

"OOGA, BOOGA. BOOGA, OOGA!"

The enthusiasm for Alice's dumb suggestion made Micki want to jump up and scream. This was just like her class! Coming up with an idea and getting carried away before they'd really thought it over. No wonder they'd been infamous at Portola. Whitney Hain already thought they were morons. Even Jason looked like he was ready to pack it in.

"I can't believe this," Micki muttered.

"What, Micki?" Bets was turned backward, agreeing with some girls behind her that a haunted house was a terrific idea.

Micki knew her class was about to blow this, and she had to set things right. Her hand shot up, fingers reaching for the ceiling. Then she was on her feet, and her voice was coming out rapid-fire.

"Wait a second, everybody," she blurted. "Let's think about this farmhouse contest. We don't have to do what the freshmen before us did!"

The crowd rustled and heads tipped in her direction. Mr. Kane, the freshman adviser, looked surprised.

Micki nervously cleared her throat and then made herself go on. "If we won the contest, we could make it much better than a haunted house. We could make it something that would last much longer, something that this school really needs. Something that's really ours!"

53

"She's right."

"Yo, Mick."

"Tell it like it is!"

Micki smiled. "That's all. We should take this farmhouse thing for real. We should show everybody at this school and win that contest."

Micki sat down, but Jason immediately took up where she had left off.

"That's right, freshmen," he echoed. "And in order to win that contest you have to make a great float. And how do you get a great float? You have great spirit at the games and a great float committee." He pointed at Micki. "Michelle, how about if you organize the freshman float committee since you feel so strongly about it! All those in favor of Michelle Greene as head of your float committee say aye."

"AIIYYYEEEEEEEEE."

"All opposed."

A few whistles. One burp.

"Michelle Greene it is."

Cheers. Notebooks conking heads. Squeals.

Jason looked to Mr. Kane for approval, and the teacher nodded. "And now that that's decided," Jason boomed, "why doesn't your new committee organizer take over this meeting."

The freshmen went nuts again, and Jason looked as though he couldn't wait to get off the stage. But before he could escape, another yell leader jogged over and whispered something in his ear. Jason put his hand over the mike and argued. Finally he shook his head and limply pleaded for order. Then he resorted to shouting into the microphone.

"QUIET!!!"

The feedback boomed across the aud, and even Mr. Kane cringed and covered his face. But most of the Class of '89 laughed.

"Sorry," Jason said, exasperated. "I was just reminded that I forgot some important announcements. First, there's going to be an all-school hayride three weeks from this Saturday. The parents of Whitney and Page Hain have been kind enough to offer their vineyard. The Pep Club is providing the wagons and the sophomores are bringing the food. We appreciate the Hain family's contribution to this Redwood event."

The freshmen went wild, but Micki suddenly lost her bounce. Why was it that every time she did something terrific, Whitney and Page were right around the corner, ready to show her up?

"Take a bow, Whitney," Jason called out, as he gestured to the side of the stage.

Whitney refused to budge from her place in the corner of the stage. She merely lifted one of her pom-poms and shook it once.

Jason was still yelling into the mike. "And remember, the first J.V. game starts right after this, Varsity at seven-thirty. I want you to be there. And be Grizzlies. All right?"

"YEAHHHHHH . . . " the class shouted back, as if they finally had figured out what they were supposed to do.

"Right," Jason answered, looking more puzzled than ever. "Michelle, come on down and take over. Why don't you all move to the front rows and have a meeting." He looked around for the other cheerleaders, but they had already left the stage. "I'm outta here."

The audience erupted as freshmen bolted, shoving each other in the aisles. Micki just stood there with this falling-off-a-cliff feeling inside. Jason had left, and she hadn't been able to talk to him at all. But she didn't have time to worry about Jason. People had surrounded her . . . were pulling and tugging. And, as usual, they wanted Michelle Greene to tell them what to do.

CHAPTER

Even as Micki was desperately trying to figure out how to make the freshmen a success, there were a few freshmen who felt conspicuously left out.

One was Page Hain.

She'd been alone during the whole rally — across the hallway and behind the door of the auditorium dressing room. Page sat surrounded by her perfect reflection on two sides, along with three open purses, four tubes of lipstick, and school books belonging to five cheerleaders.

"Hello," she whispered to herself in the mirror. "Isn't high school wonderful?"

Suddenly the door rocketed open, and Page tried to look relaxed. The tiny dressing room filled with blue and red skirts, rustling paper, huffs, and sighs, and the slightest scent of perspiration. Page guarded her eyes with her hands as Whitney and the others collected at the mirror and threw their pom-poms in her direction.

"Hi, Whitney. How did it go?"

"Don't ask."

"Was it that bad?"

"Worse."

"But I could hear the cheering from back here."

"Page, trust me. It sucked."

Page didn't push things any further, even though she was very curious. It was, after all, her class out there in the aud. But Whitney had made her position perfectly clear throughout this first week. No matter how Page argued or reasoned, the Class of '89 didn't count.

"Ugghh." Whitney's friend Ann groaned in agreement. "Can you believe how weird those kids are?"

"Tell me about it."

"Never again."

"Freshmen. Pu-leeze."

The five cheerleaders stared in the mirror, examining the damage done to their faces by the heat and the exertion and thirty minutes of aggravation. Page watched them. "What happened?" she asked in wonder.

"I told you, don't ask." Whitney found her purse on the counter and angrily foraged through it. "Page, where's my perfume? I told you not to use my perfume."

"I don't like perfume."

"Well, where is it?"

Page considered telling her sister that the canister of Yves St. Laurent was under the chair, and had been there since Whitney'd knocked over her purse, storming out to do the first cheer. But after only one week at Redwood, she didn't want to start some huge scene. So she fetched the perfume and handed it over. "Here." She felt like the cheerleading equivalent of a bat boy.

"Thank you." Whitney sprayed, and Ann lit a cigarette.

Page coughed and looked back over her shoulder toward the entrance to the auditorium. "Maybe they weren't sure what they were supposed to do," she suggested.

Whitney glowered. "Page, spare me."

"Why?"

"Don't get all offended, dear sister, but the last thing we need right now is your opinion. Just relax."

The other girls giggled and agreed.

Page wondered why they *didn't* want her opinion. After all, she was the only freshman in this group. She'd started this week with a positive outlook. But each day she'd been feeling as if she was getting pushed farther and farther into a corner. She knew that if she dared to push back, Whitney would shove even harder until Page was down and she needed Whitney to pull her up again. It had been happening all her life.

Whitney was always ahead of her, always more "grown-up," always teasing Page and making her crazy. Their older sister Julianne was just as bad. It seemed like her sisters were always waving some carrot directly in front of Page's nose, only to jerk it away at the moment it was in reach. And now it seemed as if this whole first week was a big test to see if Page could keep in line.

Whitney started to dab her cheek with a

Kleenex. "When I talked my father into letting the school use our vineyard," she complained to her friends, "I had no idea I was getting myself into this. I knew the freshmen were going to be bad, but not that bad. Maybe I could still flirt Mr. Tomasino into canceling by just smiling and telling him what a wonderful, adorable principal he is."

"Well, why don't you?" demanded Ann.

Whitney made a face as though something disgusting had just risen from the sink. "Because then I'd have to okay it with Mrs. Wong, and you know how she is about keeping your stupid commitments."

"Oh, Whitney. Isn't there some way to get out of it?"

"Not now."

"Couldn't we say it was a mistake, and the freshmen aren't really included?"

Whitney pitched the perfume into her purse. "Forget it. Stupid Jason won't let us do anything that would offend anyone at this school. After losing almost every football game last year, he's totally paranoid that no one will care this year at all."

"What if the team this year is just as bad?"

"I don't even want to think about it."

There was a collective groan as the cheerleaders stared into the mirror to blush and brush. Page couldn't help glancing at her own pale reflection. Her face was so close to the glass she could see each strand of long, dark hair; each tiny pore of fine, smooth skin. But, unlike the cheerleaders, she got no satisfaction from looking at herself. Maybe that was because other people made such a fuss over the way she looked. They stared. They made assumptions — at least that's what had happened at Oakwood. Page was never sure what it was that kids assumed. She just knew that the assumption had very little to do with how confused and left out she often felt inside.

The older girls jabbered on.

"All Mr. School Spirit Jason cares about is being the center of attention and getting the most people to cheer with him at the games."

"I know, Whitney. He doesn't care how humiliating something is for the rest of us."

"He won't face the fact that some people just don't matter!"

Page touched her cheek as the girls ignored her. She was only looking at herself to make sure that she'd really made it to high school. Whitney insisted that her friends were the only girls in Redwood worth knowing. And they were exactly the people who made Page feel as if she wasn't worth a thing.

"Come on, let's go," Whitney decided, collecting her things and heading for the door. "We have to go smile at Mr. Ritchie and tell him how handsome he is, so he'll make more posters for tonight. And I need to get home in time to shower and totally start over before the game."

"Me, too."

"Let's hit it."

They bustled out, but Page stayed huddled in the corner. She was surprised when, in the doorway, her sister remembered her and turned back. "Page, come on."

"What?"

"We're leaving. What is it?" Whitney put on her baby voice. "Are you pouting?"

"No." Page looked away, trying to ignore her sister. She was faced with her own reflection again. Why wouldn't Whitney drop this fake protective sister thing and let Page deal with high school on her own? "I have to go to my locker."

"All right," Whitney sighed. "Meet us in the parking lot in fifteen minutes." She started to leave, then turned back and checked one of her Swatches. "Ann's doing you a favor by driving. Don't be late."

Page didn't move until she heard the last aerobic shoe shuffle down the hallway. Finally she slipped down from the counter, gathered her books, and eager to escape from the smoke and the smell of makeup, hurried out.

Five minutes later, Page still felt coiled up inside. " 'Ann's doing you a favor. Don't be late,' " Page mimicked, padding down the hall. "I'm sure you'll miss me so much. Who will you push around if I'm not there?"

She was heading for her locker, even though she didn't really need to go there. She wasn't sure where to go. She wondered why she'd made such a big deal out of getting away from Whitney, when now she would only go to the parking lot and wait for her. Then she'd sit in the car while the other girls gossiped and laughed about things that Page didn't understand.

"Ha ha ha," Page mumbled to herself again.

She was answered by laughter. Real, goofy,

awkward laughter. Drawn by it, Page turned back toward the auditorium. The door that led backstage was propped open. The laughter was leaping out of it.

Hugging her books to her plain cotton shirt, Page tiptoed through the door, up three steps, and into the dusty, dark backstage. She stood just behind the teaser curtain, hidden by the green velvet, holding back a sneeze. Her class was still there. The class that she was part of and yet felt as far away from as if she were an exchange student from Mars.

A boy in overalls and a baseball cap was describing his vision for a homecoming float — a caveman in a cage with a grizzly bear hitting a hammer that in turn opened the cage. Everyone laughed and Page couldn't help laughing, too. But then she sucked her laughter back in and wondered if anyone had heard her.

She felt almost as if she was spying, as if her classmates were the ones onstage, and she was in the audience. She stared at the back of the girl at the helm: the explosion of energy, pink jeans, cropped blue sweater, one foot excitedly slipping in and out of a dark loafer. Michelle Greene. From Page's gym class. A shudder went through Page as she remembered that awful scene with Michelle and Whitney in the caf on Monday.

Suddenly the laughter erupted again and shiny soap bubbles were floating and diving over the first few rows. The freshmen twisted and turned, but no one could tell who had the container of soap or the bubble wand. Kids squirmed and swiveled as big glistening ovals bounced off their noses and the tops of their heads. When a huge bubble exploded — unnoticed — on the back of Mr. Kane's neck, Page busted up, doubling over, and letting out a hearty, low laugh.

When she was finished, it seemed as if the entire class was staring up at her. Somehow Page wasn't behind the curtain anymore, but standing at the edge of the stage, reaching for a fat, drifting soap bubble. Page froze. The bubble sank, hit the floor, and splattered into nothingness.

"You're a little late," Micki said.

Page wasn't sure what to do. She'd gone from nonexistence to a starring role in a matter of seconds. Both parts were equally terrifying.

"I'm sorry. I'm just passing through," she said, forcing herself to sound calm.

"Well, pass through then," Micki offered. "Do not pass Go. Do not collect two hundred dollars." A few kids laughed at Micki's joke.

Page nodded and scurried off the stage. But as she headed down the aisle, Amy Cuddy, who was in her history class, waved her over. At the same time two boys from geometry popped up.

"Page!" Amy whispered. "Here's a seat."

The boys shuffled and moved over. "There's one here," they beckoned.

Micki was still watching her. "Page, would you like to join us? We are involved in important decisions here. The future of a caveman and a bear are at stake."

Page still stood in the aisle. Kids were gawking at her, the way they always seemed to gawk at her face and her hair and her clothes. Even those diamond earrings her mother had given her seemed too pretentious, and Page had ended up wearing only one, and substituting the other with a dime-store earring made of glass. She felt as if she were being swallowed up by people's eyes, and she wanted to yell, *WHY! What do you see in me? Tell me, so maybe I can see it, too!* Feeling her face redden, she scampered even faster, not looking back until she shoved the metal bar and escaped into the lobby.

When she got there, her heart was throbbing. She folded down to the cool linoleum floor because she wanted to yell, and she knew she didn't dare open her mouth. She let out a tiny cry, then breathed it back in when she heard the flap of a page being turned.

She looked up. There was another girl sitting in the lobby. She was in the corner, drawing in a large sketch pad, stretched out as if she'd been there for a while. Page recognized her from gym class, the same gym class she shared with Michelle Greene. She knew the girl's name. Laurel Griffith. Page remembered everyone's name.

"Is something wrong?" Laurel asked right away. She slipped off her glasses and observed Page with eyes so green and intense that Page thought of X rays, or those fake, colored contact lenses. And yet, there was nothing about Laurel that seemed dangerous or phony.

Page didn't answer. She was afraid her entire family history would come out. She was afraid she would spew out all her frustration about high school until Laurel would snub her, too.

Laurel watched her a few more seconds, then went back to her sketch pad.

Page wanted to yell, *Yes, something's wrong. High school's wrong. Everything's wrong!* She wanted to walk over and sit close to Laurel, close to someone. Just one friend who knew what it was like to be on your own. Instead, she took a breath and didn't say a word. When Laurel looked at her agan, Page got up quickly and hurried away.

CHAPTER 7

It worked.

The planet project was a *huge* success. The spinning Mercury and Venus and Jupiter just about put the whole school in orbit. Even Mr. Dunbrick had to admit that it was one of the most interesting combinations of class teamwork and scientific data that he'd ever seen at Redwood, and Principal Tomasino suggested taking the model and putting it into the glass display booth near the entrance of the school. For their contributions, John Pryble, Paul O'Conner, and Sarah Parker got strokes from Micki, and just about everyone else, for figuring out the mechanics of the beast. The freshmen as a whole were beginning to get noticed. Micki felt proud.

But she also felt the need to do something bigger and better. The science project had shown the way. She'd managed to talk the same team that had put together the planets into working on the homecoming float. Around the theme of "Cage the Cavemen," John and Paul and Sarah and several others were beginning to gather materials, do preliminary sketches, and think about how to make it all work. Meanwhile Bets was encouraging them with homemade muffins, and Doug was toying with the idea of a musical theme.

But Micki knew that she was one who had to keep it together. That was why that Thursday afternoon in gym class, she was ready to go outside and run all the pressure off. She was looking forward to a good game of soccer out in the fresh Redwood Hills fall air. Inside the locker room it was stuffy and crowded. You could hear other girls' conversations a long way.

"I heard she's a model," someone was gossiping.

"Amy, that's not true. The agency in San Francisco wanted her to be a model, but she wouldn't do it."

"Honest?"

"That's what I heard. That's what Carlos told me."

"He did?"

"Yeah, well, Carlos. He's in love with her. He keeps talking about how he's dying to sit next to her on the hayride. Page Hain, that's all he thinks about."

"I think he actually talked to her."

"Nobody's talked to her."

"That's not true, either. Cindy talked to her in history class. She said Page was nice. She wasn't snobby at all."

"I wonder who'll ask her to the Homecoming Dance?"

"Jason Sandy?"

"Maybe Nick Rhodes."

"Ohhhh."

Micki was perched on the wooden gym bench, pulling on her soccer cleats, while Bets sat next to her, rolling up the sleeves of a gray Redwood sweatshirt. Micki felt as if her ears were two radar dishes, and unfortunately she was picking up information she didn't want to be tuned in to. Especially that last tidbit about Jason Sandy, and Nick Rhodes — a sophomore jock whom every girl in school was wild about. Overhearing her classmates, who were dressing in the next aisle, gave her an itchy, pent-up feeling inside.

"Why does everybody talk about her all the time?" Micki took one of Peter's old ties out of her book bag. She used it to tie back her hair during PE.

"Who?" Bets was working on her braids.

"Page."

"Oh."

"She hasn't done anything," Micki reasoned. "She hardly talks to anyone. What do people see in her?"

Bets leaned over her long freckled legs to look up and down the aisle. Page's locker was way at the end of the row, but they usually didn't see her until they were all out on the field. Cindy White said Page always snuck off behind the showers to change so no one could stare at her. "Lots of people like her . . . um, they think she's something special . . . I guess."

"Do they?" Micki took one of her deep breaths. She'd been getting this feeling lately when she saw Page at school or heard people talking about her. Micki figured the feeling had started that first day in the lunchroom. It had certainly gotten stronger at the spirit rally when Page had stumbled in, made a scene, and then walked out without even offering to help. And the part that was really getting hard to swallow was that as time went on, some kids had started to idolize Page. It was as if she were some kind of princess or movie star, and the fact that she didn't lift a finger to help her class didn't seem to matter.

Micki stood up and shook her arms and legs, trying to fling this feeling away. She told herself that Page wasn't important. Especially compared to the terrific success her class had just had with their planet project. She pulled Bets to her feet. "Are you glad we start soccer today?"

"Yes," Bets smiled. Bets was a terrific soccer player and probably one of the best athletes in the whole freshman class.

They shut their lockers and went over to the mirror to finish dressing. "Mary Beth Dubrosky was complaining about soccer," Micki told Bets. "She wanted more coed running. I told her that two weeks of running was enough for me."

Pink spread over Bets's face until her freckles almost disappeared. She leaned in toward Micki and whispered, "You know why she was complaining?"

They both started giggling. "I know. She likes watching the boys."

70

"You should hear her talk about Paul. It's gross."

"Paul O'Conner? No!"

"Yes!"

"PAUL!"

They hooted until they almost cried. This was one of Micki's favorite things about Bets. If the mood was right, they could become a pair of hopeless gigglers in about two seconds. And Micki's mood was right today. That pent-up feeling was an easy gateway to any other intense emotion.

"I mean, um," Bets panted, wiping tears, "I like watching boys. . . . But she's, you know, serious about it."

Micki was still laughing. She and Bets had this boy conversation a lot. She usually got the feeling that Bets was trying to figure things out, but for now she was just fine without a boyfriend, thank you. "Do you think you'll go to the homecoming dance?"

Bets shrugged. "I don't know. I guess you're supposed to have a date. Doug keeps talking about going."

"Doug?" Micki started giggling again. Sometimes she caught Doug looking at Bets in the dreamiest way. But Doug was pretty hard to take seriously, and besides, she didn't think Bets ever thought about him as anything but a friend.

Bets moved back to let other girls get close to the mirror. Then she jumped up, hung from the chin bar Mrs. Lucht had put in front of the doorway, and did a chin-up. For such a slender girl, Bets was amazingly strong. "What about you?"

Micki joined Bets in the doorway. "I want to make it through the hayride first. Then I'll think about homecoming." She looked out the door at the basketball courts. Two boys were playing one-on-one. The air smelled of wood smoke, and the playing fields were bordered with fallen leaves. They walked out.

"You'll probably be picked captain," Bets said, following Micki and ducking under a volleyball net. "You'd better, um, pick me first for your team."

"Who else would I pick first?" Micki stopped and turned back to face Bets. "How come you're never the captain? You dribbled better than anyone when we practiced."

Bets shook her head. "I could never be captain."

"Why. . . ?" Suddenly Micki's vioce trailed off. A leggy girl was running over the basketball courts, heading right for them on her way to the gym. The gait was awkward, the clothes were plain, the face was unmistakably stunning. It was Page.

"Speak of the devil," Micki whispered to Bets. They both stopped on the volleyball court and started stretching.

Page was in a hurry, but when she passed Micki and Bets she slowed down. Finally she turned and jogged back to them. Her gray eyes had that Hain iciness mixed with something else that was cloudy and hidden. Micki couldn't read her.

"Hi," Page said in a noncommittal voice. There was a long pause while the girls stood there, staring at the asphalt and kicking fallen leaves.

"I heard about your project," Page finally went on.

"You did?"

"Yes." She kicked leaves again. "How's the float going?"

"Fine. You ready for the hayride in another week?"

Page nodded. She started to go, then turned back. "So the float's going okay?"

Suddenly Bets was nudging Micki, and Micki knew what she had to do. Bets was made of sympathy. She was telling Micki to invite Page to join on the float, which at the moment was the last thing Micki wanted to do. Micki cleared her throat. "So, do you want to work on the float with us?" she asked in a stiff voice.

Page's gray eyes opened wider, as if she were in shock. For a moment she just stood there, but then this phony "social girl" laugh came out of her. "Oh, no," she said. "Whitney says let other people work on the freshman float. She says it's yucky work."

That feeling came boiling back inside Micki. "Fine with me," she answered.

Page frowned, hesitated, then raced into the gym.

Micki turned to Bets. "Can you believe that?"

"I know," Bets sympathized.

Micki leaned her head back and gave one groan to the clear fall sky. Then she tapped Bets's arm. "Let's go play soccer," she urged. "I really feel like kicking something today."

A few minutes later, everybody was ready to play. They were all in a circle at the goal line, with the single exception of Laurel Griffith. As usual, Laurel was alone at the fence, staring off at the mountains. Bets thought it was weird the way Laurel stood back every day, never talking to anyone. It was the third week of school, and Laurel didn't seem to want to join anything. Bets instinctively moved closer to Micki and the other girls, who were stamping their feet and making little clouds of vapor as they talked.

"So it's going to be 'Cage the Cavemen' " Micki was saying. "We'll have a caveman locked up — probably Doug — in furs. Can you believe that, Doug in furs?"

"I can."

"Me, too."

Micki was instantly back in fine form, joking about the cavemen and how building the float was going to be a real challenge. The girls were all attention, laughing at everything Micki said, until Alice Dubrosky pointed out that Mrs. Lucht was finally heading over with her clipboard and a soccer ball. The girls all turned to look and the conversation stopped. Page accompanied their gym teacher. The girls gawked shamelessly.

"Well, that's one way to get out of a tardy mark," Micki commented; "make sure the teacher is as late as you are."

Nobody laughed, even though Bets had heard rumors of how the Hain sisters were pros at kissing up to teachers. Now even Bets was starting to get annoyed at how unfair it was to put Page on a pedestal.

"Can you believe someone can look like that in a sweatshirt and gym shorts?" sighed Amy Cuddy, a girl on the float committee.

"She has incredible style. Totally simple. I love those two different earrings."

"Well, I heard," Amy announced in a pointed whisper, "that nobody will beat her for homecoming princess."

Micki suddenly looked as if someone had dropped an anvil on her toe. The other girls were too preoccupied with envy to notice Micki's expression. But it filled Bets with concern . . . and outrage. How dare these girls get more excited about Page's stupid earrings than about Micki's planet project or the float? She nudged Micki's tennis shoe. "You okay?"

Micki took in a big breath and tried to smile. "Fine."

Micki didn't look okay, and Bets knew it was her job to make her feel better. For once Bets took the floor and her voice came out loud and clear. "Page Hain sure likes kissing up to Lucht," Bets said, glancing back at the field. "I guess she wants an A in PE."

Amy was still gawking. "I bet she will be our homecoming princess. I can't imagine who could beat her."

"Well, I just hope Page doesn't have to run onto the field if she gets elected," Bets blurted. Her tongue felt like twisted twine again, which was what usually happened when she had to talk in front of people. Nevertheless, Micki was at stake here, so Bets forged ahead. "I just mean . . . Page isn't perfect," she stammered. "She runs funny . . . like some of the guys on our football team."

Everybody looked at Page and then someone started to snicker. Page *did* run as if her feet were way too big, just like a few guys on their losing football team. It looked pretty geeky.

"She runs like a duck," said Micki with a grateful smile to Bets.

The girls continued to stare as Page jogged closer.

"Quack quack," giggled Mary Beth.

Cindy White imitated Page, flapping her feet as they all shushed and tittered their way into line for roll.

Page ignored them and fell in on the other side of Laurel Griffith, who finally took her place next to Micki. There were a few muffled giggles, then Mrs. Lucht began calling roll. The teacher set down her clipboard and kicked the ball onto the field. "You all remember the rules?" she asked them.

"YES, MRS. LUCHT!" More giggles.

"Cut the jokes and pick captains."

"How about Micki?" Bets said right away. Micki stepped forward and was unanimously approved. But when the next captain was selected that anvil-on-the-toe expression returned to Micki's face.

"Page Hain," pronounced Amy. Page frowned, as if she was confused rather than flattered. In spite of that, she was confirmed as quickly as Micki.

"Pick your teams, girls," Mrs. Lucht ordered. "Micki, go first."

Micki selected Bets, then Bets stood at her side, waiting to see who Page would pick. She expected it to be Amy, who'd nominated Page, or Mary Beth, who was the best goalie.

"Laurel Griffith." Page chose in an unsure voice.

Laurel Griffith? New-girl Laurel who didn't seem interested in Micki or the float or anything about their class? Bets was baffled.

So was Laurel. "Me?" Her blonde head tipped up and her glasses slid down to the tip of her nose. When Page didn't answer, Laurel took her place at Page's side. The choosing went on, one by one, until even the girls who couldn't kick a beach ball were on a team.

"All right, girls. Let's play!"

The teams spread out across the field. Micki set the ball for the first kick. As the ball went into play, Micki took off. She went right for Page Hain — hair flying, feet stabbing, Micki out of control.

The ball skitted but Page managed to stop it dead. She guarded it with her heel and glared at Micki. Red covered her cheeks like paint. When Micki tried to kick it again, Page scooped up the ball with her palm and started in the other direction.

"HANDS!" Micki screamed.

"That's right. HANDS!" Bets heard herself yell at almost the same time.

Page threw her arms over her head in fury, then grabbed the ball and hugged it. She wouldn't toss it to Mrs. Lucht until the teacher had blown her whistle three times.

Things seemed to calm down a little after that. Once she'd reminded the girls about penalties, Mrs. Lucht tossed the ball to Bets and told her to put it into play. Bets knew she had to get it to Alice or Micki, and was looking for them on the field, when Laurel Griffith came bearing down on her. She had taken off her glasses and her hair was twisted in a sloppy ponytail. Her green eyes were fixed on Bets, and she was coming straight toward the ball.

Bets kicked. She kicked the ball hard so that it skipped on the grass and shot up, almost into Laurel's face. Laurel jumped back while Micki cut in front, intercepting it, and taking off. Now it was Page hounding Micki, darting her feet in Micki's path, hovering and elbowing. Laurel joined her, skirting on the other side of Micki. She also stabbed with her feet, and Micki was pinned in.

"Kick it, Mick. Kick it to me!" hollered Mary Beth, who was near the goal, completely unguarded.

But Micki could barely move. Page and Laurel both were swiping at her, aiming more for Micki's shins than the ball. Bets wasn't sure what to do, but then she was running. With the full force of her strong body, she knocked Page back, then stuck out a foot to trip Laurel. All three of them smacked down on the grass. Page grabbed Micki's ankle and she tumbled, too, landing with a thud and a shriek of pain.

"HOLD IT!" Mrs. Lucht yelled, so loudly it made Bets wince. "What's gotten into you girls?

What do you think this is, wrestling? Laps. All four of you."

The girls got up slowly, glaring at one another, ignoring the scrapes and grass burns on their hands and knees.

Mrs. Lucht shook her head. "LAPS. GET GOING!"

Micki raced toward the baseball diamond, while Page took off the other way, and Laurel jogged aimlessly along the fence. Bets didn't move. She couldn't quite absorb what had happened . . . that she had knocked Page and Laurel down. She hadn't done anything like that since she was nine and her little brother had pulled the arms off her dolls. She stared blankly until Mrs. Lucht yelled, "BETSY FRANK, START RUNNING. YOU KNOW BETTER THAN TO PLAY LIKE THAT!"

Bets ran. Her embarrassment stung harder than her scraped palm or her bruised shin. Of course she knew better. She knew better than to hurt people for no reason. Too humiliated to look back, Bets ran faster and faster until she caught up to Micki and followed her around the field.

Two sides. . . .

One day after the soccer fiasco, another kind of game was being held between different opponents — the Mendocino Braves and the Redwood Grizzlies. It was being held in the afternoon because the Braves had to travel over a hundred miles to play. None of that really mattered to Laurel Griffith. She wasn't interested in where the teams were from, but only in how they would look on paper.

She pictured both teams. Lined up. Crouched. Bands of black under their eyes and macho scowls. That image in mind, she went back to her pad on the easel and began to draw.

"There," she whispered to her cartoon, urging it to come to life. "You start on that side." She put a chalky finger to her lips. "And don't tell anyone I'm here." She breathed in the art room smells — paint and clay and the oily chalk on her hands. As usual, she was alone.

Almost everyone was over at the stadium. The student body still had hope, even though the Grizzlies had been slaughtered in their first two games. The banners and posters said this game was going to turn things around, and Laurel's father used the same argument. He insisted she go to the game. Laurel had wanted to tell him that she had practically given up on Redwood. She didn't care if they turned things around . . . or inside out or upside down. As usual, she'd said nothing.

But by the final bell, Laurel knew she couldn't face it. She was at her locker and she knew that Mr. Ritchie's art room door was open. Old habits died hard. She snuck in. Blinds down. Lights on. Door locked. Easel up, and it was almost like being back in San Jose.

"MINE!" Laurel squiggled out of the mouth of one of her figures, a girl with too much energy and vicious feet. Laurel had colored her cheeks bright red and made her open mouth too large for her face. She added a supporting team, all smaller versions of Micki Greene. Then she sketched herself in: round glasses; yellow hair; long, lacy dress. Laurel gave herself a team. Just one or two girls. That strange boy Jed she'd met the first day. And a forgiving angel made of three powder-blue stars.

POWIE! fought one side. ZOWIE! ZAP! responded the other in block, graffiti-type letters. Laurel kept sketching. The battle was on. Laurel versus her new life at Redwood High.

She was expanding her forces, taking over new territories of pinks and reds, when a key slid into the art room door. Laurel froze, startled, as if she'd been suddenly awakened from a deep, dreamy snooze. The door swung open and stadium noise rumbled in — far-off groans of disappointment. A man wearing a cardigan sweater and plaid stretch slacks was standing in the doorway. Laurel thought first of her father and felt guilty. But it wasn't her father. It was Mr. Ritchie, one of the art teachers.

"How'd you get in here?"

"It was open."

Confused, he squinted back at the door. "Are you in my second-period Art One? Fourth?"

"I'm in Mrs. Foley's class. Laurel Griffith." Laurel turned her sketch away so he couldn't see it. But her effort was probably unnecessary. From what she'd heard, Mr. Ritchie was only interested in upperclass hall murals and posters for the pep rallies.

"So what are you doing here? I didn't say you could come in here after school and, work." He scratched his head. He was bald on top with wispy fringe. "Did I?"

"No."

"Well, you can't just come in here because I forgot to lock up," Mr. Ritchie huffed. "You should be at the game. Not that it's any better than last year, but you should be there. Are you a freshman?"

"I wanted to draw."

"Pretty nervy of a freshman to come in here without permission."

Laurel thought of asking why a freshman should be any less nervy than anyone else at this school, but instead she gave up. It wasn't worth the hassle. Next time she'd sneak in somewhere else and hope that she didn't get caught. She flipped her sketch pad closed . . . didn't say a word. No talk, no confrontation. But suddenly she had to stop because there was another person in the doorway, a person who made Laurel want to talk, or at least ask a few questions.

"Hello."

It was Page Hain. Laurel hadn't spoken to Page since that weird soccer game yesterday. Page wore a plain khaki jumper, and her earrings sparkled: one blue, one white. Mr. Ritchie was gazing at Page's face so intently that he certainly didn't notice that her earrings were different colors, or that Laurel had stopped putting her things away.

Page glanced briefly, nervously, at Laurel, then approached the art teacher. "You must be Mr. Ritchie," she said with a stuck-on smile. Her coy tone surprised Laurel, just as Page had surprised her by picking her first for her soccer team.

"That's me." He neatened his wispy hair.

Page hesitated, as if she were figuring out just how to do this. When she spoke, her tone was a stream of sugary smoke. It sounded false, almost as if it were coming from someone else. "I'm Page Hain. Whitney's little sister. Whitney told me how much you've been helping the cheerleaders. She says you did all the best posters yourself. She says they couldn't have done anything this year without you."

"She did?" Mr. Ritchie was devouring Page's flattery in one greedy gulp.

"Oh, yes. She said I have to take your class next year."

Even Laurel had overheard kids gossiping about Page. Some insisted that Page was a kiss-up snob, while others acted as if she were a humble goddess. Until this moment Laurel suspected that Page was just an outsider like herself.

Page went on. "Anyway, since I want to take your class later, I thought maybe I could sit in here with Laurel so she could show me some things about drawing. Just until the game ends. That is, if it's okay with you."

"Well." He glanced at Laurel, then back at Page. He softened. "I guess I shouldn't stifle any creative impulses. Okay. You two can stay here — but only until the game's over and I come back and lock up."

"Thank you, Mr. Ritchie."

His eyes still stuck on Page, Mr. Ritchie found more keys in his desk, waved, and walked out. " 'Bye."

After he left, Laurel said nothing. Moans of defeat wafted over from the football field until Page closed the door and it was quiet. Pleased with herself, Page hiked herself up and sat on a table.

Laurel was very confused. Yesterday in gym she'd suspected that Page was the one girl at Redwood with whom she had something in common. Now she feared that the worst rumors about Page were true. She wrapped herself in a sheet of invisible waxed paper — an undetectable shield that kept people away. Page Hain was the type of girl you needed protection from. As if she were alone again, Laurel flipped her sketch pad open and went back to her cartoon.

"Hhhuh," Page huffed audibly. Her satisfaction wilted as Laurel continued to ignore her. Finally she slid off the table, wrapped her arms around herself, and started to wander around the room as if she were at a museum. "You're welcome," she muttered sarcastically.

"What?"

"You could say thanks." Now Page's voice was unsure, as it had been when she'd picked Laurel for her team. She stopped strolling and repeated, "You could say thank you."

"What for?" Laurel concentrated on her drawing. She'd just realized that a figure on her side of the battle wore one blue earring and one white one. She considered rubbing the figure out. She didn't.

"Well, excuse me for trying to help." Page flapped her arms against her sides. "I was at my locker outside and I heard Ritchie hassling you. I was trying to thank you for taking my side in soccer. I thought maybe you didn't want to have to go to the football game."

"Why would I care about football?"

"Everybody cares about stupid football. Oh, forget it." Page headed for the door, then turned back. "Besides, the day of the spirit rally, you were hiding in the lobby. You didn't want to be there, either."

Laurel stared at her drawing, shading in meaningless red slants across the background, barely seeing the pad. "I wasn't hiding."

"Oh, right. You were just sitting on the floor by yourself because it's so comfortable."

Laurel's hand began to tremble. The waxed paper was coming loose. "I was drawing."

"In the aud lobby? I mean, excuse me for being so observant, but I figured that maybe you didn't really want to be at that rally."

"Why would you think that?" Laurel finally lifted her eyes.

Page's cheeks were flushed with frustration. "Because *I* didn't want to be there! And now everybody's at the game, and I figured you didn't want to be at the game because I know *I* don't want to be at the game. But if that's not right, just forget it. I never should have started this. Never, never, ever!" She put her hand over her face. "I never should have gotten into this at all. I'm sorry." She started for the door.

"What are you talking about?" Laurel came away from behind her easel.

Page looked different. Anger distorted her perfect features. She waved her hands as though she were trying to fling them away. "Forget it. I'm sure you think I'm awful just like everyone else does. You think I'm a snob and a kiss-up just like my sisters."

"Well, you did just kiss up to Ritchie."

"AAAGGGHH," Page exploded. "Excuse me, but I didn't know how else to do it! I keep doing that because I don't know how else to act. I thought maybe because you didn't go to the same

86

middle school with everyone like me, that maybe you were different. But I was wrong!" She was on her way out, her hand on the doorknob.

Laurel wasn't sure what was happening. She just knew that her giving up, caving-in point had passed, but somehow she was still in this fight. The effort made scary tears push against her throat. She didn't cry. She prided herself in never crying. Almost never. "Page."

Page stopped. Her forehead thunked against the door. "Forget it."

"What?"

"I apologize. I'm yelling at the wrong person. Forget I said anything."

"It's okay."

"No, it isn't."

"It is."

"Why?"

"I don't know. But it is."

Page stood awkwardly, as if she wanted to leave but her arms and legs wouldn't obey her. Finally she collapsed into the nearest chair. "I hate high school. I hate being a freshman."

Laurel's tears pressed again. She strong-armed them back. "I know how you feel."

"No, you don't. Everybody thinks I'm just like my sisters. And maybe I am. Maybe I will turn out to be like my stupid sisters. Yesterday Micki Greene asked me to work on the freshman float and I didn't know what to say, so I answered her just like my sisters would've." Page buried her face in her hands. Finally she looked up. "Do you think I'm just like them?"

"I don't know. I guess you don't have to be."

Page had picked up tempera paint from the tabletop. Blue was smeared like war paint across her cheek. "I'm sorry. I'm horrible when I get mad like that."

"That's okay." Laurel slowly approached the table. "I don't get so mad about it, but I know what it's like."

"What?"

"I know what it's like to feel that way."

Page looked up at her, her eyes needy and full of warmth. "Everybody talks about me," she explained. "Yesterday in gym they were making fun of the way I run. They thought I didn't know, but I did. Then today, I went to the game because Whitney said I had to, and these boys I don't even know moved all their books and made this huge deal out of wanting me to sit with them. And they all were laughing and whispering. Can't people treat me like a normal human?"

"Normal?" Laurel sat down next to her. It felt a little like old times, with her two friends in San Jose. Advising. Comforting. Talking. "I don't know anybody normal. Do you?"

Page thought about it and started to smile. "I don't think so."

"I don't know very many people."

Page wrinkled her nose. "I do."

Suddenly Laurel began to chuckle, very softly. "What's so funny?"

"I just thought of something." She looked away. "Do you want to see what I'm drawing?"

Page jumped up and cried, "Yes!"

Head down, silky hair over her face, Laurel

led Page over to the easel. She waited, nervous, while Page looked.

"That's fantastic! That's amazing. You really drew that?"

Laurel nodded, pride blooming inside.

"Is that me?" Page gasped, pointing to the figure with the two different earrings.

"Maybe."

"Who's that?" Page surprised Laurel by pointing to the figure representing Jed. "Do I know him?"

"I doubt it. He's just some guy." Laurel pointed instead to the girl with the big mouth. "Do you know who that is?"

"MICHELLE GREENE!" they said at the same time.

"Now, she sure didn't act normal yesterday," said Page and they both laughed.

"And that's you," Page pointed out.

With terrific speed, Laurel colored in her and Page's faces with green and magenta.

Page giggled. "Aliens," he said.

Laurel drew huge antennae and cones on the tops of their heads. "Visitors from strange lands."

"I know!" Page grabbed a piece of yellow chalk and scribbled big, webbed feet on her picture. "There. Now I'm really a duck, just like they said." Laurel laughed, too, and tried to take the chalk away. But Page kept it and drew duck feet on Laurel's figure, too."

"Oh, no," Laurel laughed. "Not me, too!"

They were both grabbing at the chalk now.

Puffs of magenta and green dotted their faces and their clothes. When Page started to go off on another laughing jag, she put her hands to her cheeks. When she took them off she looked like something dressed up for Halloween.

Laurel pointed at her and howled. "Look at you!"

Page scurried to the mirror over the sink. Laurel joined her, adding a few more swipes of chalk to Page's jumper and to her own faded lavender dress. They were giggling now, leaning on each other helplessly. "Maybe you should look like that the night of the hayride!"

The laughter ended. There was just the tick of the wall clock and the announcer at the football game sounding very far away. "I was thinking of running away from home that night," Page said dully. "If people think I'm a freak now, just wait until they all see where I live. Are you going?"

"Me?"

"I didn't think so."

"No way."

"Are you sure?"

Laurel nodded and they were quiet again. Page played with a stick of chalk while Laurel stared at her sketch pad.

"Maybe you can get out of it," Laurel finally suggested. "You could come over to my house that night. I'm sure my dad wouldn't mind."

"I have to go." Page paused. "But you could come early and we could just hang out. Maybe we won't have to ride on the wagons."

"I didn't sign up."

"Please. I'm sure you could be my guest."

Laurel wanted that safe waxed-paper wrapping again. Without it, she felt like a bruised piece of fruit in danger of being thrown away. And yet, there was something in Page's gray eyes that she didn't want to turn down. Friendship. "I'm not sure. I guess it would mean a lot to my dad if I went."

"It would mean a lot to me."

"It would?"

Page nodded, a little embarrassed.

Close, important friendship. The only kind that Laurel considered worth having. Laurel extended her chalk-covered hand. "I guess I can stand it. I've sure been through worse. Okay."

"Oh, thanks." Page glowed. "Just you and me."

"Us against the rest of them."

They shook hands and started to laugh again.

CHAPTER 9

In the next week, the week before the hayride, it started to rain. Pure, unpredictable Redwood Hills October rain. The leaves were prematurely blown off their trees and made the one-year-old campus look matted and waterlogged. The rain frizzed Micki's hair and ruined Doug's band practice, but it also canceled the one part of Micki's schedule that she could not approach with her usual optimism and good humor — soccer.

The rain took care of it. On Monday it was so soggy they gave up on team sports and went inside for individual gymnastics. Micki and Bets hit the mats, while Page Hain went over to the balance beam with Laurel Griffith. For a while it looked as if the class would be split down the middle, half tumbling, half balancing. But the other girls found it hard to stay on the beam, and besides, Page and Laurel (who seemed to have become overnight friends) talked mainly to each other. Meanwhile Micki and Bets were laughing and tumbling and including everybody who joined them whether they could somersault or not. By the end of the period it was thirty-four to two — thirty-four girls on the mat (not counting Micki and Bets) and two on the beam (just Laurel and Page).

That was Monday.

Then on Tuesday afternoon, with the hayride getting so close that people hardly talked about anything else, Micki was in her kitchen at home, cramming for a science test and trying not to eat. Peter was home from college, having an emergency crisis over changing his major, and her parents were worried. No one was appreciating any of Micki's comments or jokes, when suddenly the phone rang. Every five minutes it rang again and again. Each time, it was for Micki.

Bets called from the vet's office to ask what Micki planned to wear to the hayride.

Doug called to ask why Bets wasn't home, and then played Micki a new riff on his saxophone.

Paul wanted Micki to know that he was still looking for chicken wire.

Alice and Mary Beth needed Micki's opinion on their ideas if they won the farmhouse contest — Mary Beth wanted to turn it into a disco. Alice was opting for a tutoring center.

Lastly, Carlos called to volunteer for the float committee, and Cindy invited her to a slumber party.

Suddenly Micki realized that Peter was staring

at her. Her mom and dad were staring at her. Peter broke the silence by saying, "Boy, Micki, your friends couldn't exist without you." Her dad gave her a thumbs-up and her mom smiled, as if for once they were acknowledging something important about her besides good grades and the school activities that would go on her transcripts.

Then the miracle happened. . . .

Thursday. Micki was at lunch in the future theater that was now their daily lunch place. The chatter, which was its usual freshman loud and silly, stopped. For an awful moment Micki thought it was Whitney and Page. It wasn't. It was Jason Sandy, wearing his letter sweater and a red bow tie. And he was standing right behind Micki.

Micki hadn't seen Jason since the rally, at least not more than on the field during games or passing in the hall — times when he never did more than smile his fantastic smile, pat her hair, and rush to the next admirer. Then, with Micki's heart pounding so fiercely she thought it might leap into someone's lunch, he rested his hand on her shoulder and asked if she was going on the hayride. Bets stared. The twins stared. Paul took off his baseball cap, and even Doug was impressed.

Barely breathing and almost speechless, Micki had said, yes, yes, of course! she was going on the hayride that weekend. And he said, "See you there," and smiled and walked away. That was all that happened, but that in itself was pretty wonderful.

And now, in the late afternoon on Saturday,

Micki was feeling so lucky that she couldn't quite believe it was possible for things to get even better.

She was in the parking lot, surrounded by Doug and Bets and everybody else. They all hovered around the freshman bus . . . which stood next to the sophomore bus . . . and the junior and senior buses . . . which were about to take them over to the Hain Vineyard for the first big event of Micki's high school life.

"It better not rain," Bets was saying, stamping her cowboy boots on the asphalt but missing the puddles left over from the day before. It was windy enough to make the flag snap, and the sky was so crammed with rain clouds it looked like a layer of gray mattresses. Still, not a drop of water had come down since the previous afternoon, and the forecast was for semiclear skies.

"You cold?" asked Doug.

"Brrrr," Micki and Bets chattered at the same time.

"Hey, Bets," Doug teased, bumping her with his hip, "I'll keep you warm."

Bets giggled, wrinkled her nose, and backed away, almost stumbling over his saxophone case, which was wrapped in a green Hefty bag. "What's that?"

Doug grinned and mimed a riff on his horn.

"But Doug . . . I mean, why? You're weird."

Doug gazed at her. Bets wore jeans, a western shirt, and a yellow slicker. Doug, in contrast, had on a huge suit jacket, army pants, a Woodstock T-shirt, and a green pipe cleaner twisted around his rat tail. "Like I learned in Boy Scouts. Be prepared. Just in case things get boring."

"Somehow, Doug, I can't picture you as a Boy Scout," Micki quipped and everybody laughed.

That was when Micki saw Jason again.

He was leaning against the junior bus, chatting with Gus Baldwin, captain of the football team; and the treasurer of the sophomore class, Meg McCall. Meg was tall and composed, with smooth, dark hair and dazzling long legs. But it was merely his gestures that were focused on Meg and Gus. His eyes were pinned on Micki.

Still, Micki didn't trust it. When boys stared at her, she was never sure if it meant a bug was crawling in her hair, or something from the cafeteria was stuck to her skirt. As much as she wanted to believe that a guy was interested in her, she was still a freshman. And realistically, she knew that Jason falling for her was about as likely as her mother giving up her job to sit home and watch soap operas. And yet, Jason was still staring.

Micki's blood ran faster and spurts of energy zapped her hands and the backs of her knees. Jason started to walk toward her. Hands in pockets. Wide, sure shoulders. One, two, three, four spirit buttons on his sweater. Eyes like melted chocolate kisses. Micki's knees trembled.

"Hi, Michelle," he said. Smooth. Easy.

"Hi."

He tossed his head, gesturing for her to move a few feet away from the others. She followed as if attached by wires.

96

When they were alone, his teddy bear eyes traveled from the top of her head down to her lips. She followed those eyes, unable to derail herself.

"I was wondering if you could ride on the junior bus with me?" he asked her.

Micki stared at this mouth to make sure he'd actually said it. "Is it okay?"

"Sure. Your class can get along without you."

Micki'd meant was it okay with the teachers and the juniors. And yet, now that Jason mentioned it, she realized that there was the consideration of her classmates. Knowing the freshmen, they might not even make it to the vineyard without her. But there really wasn't much point in deliberating. Jason was the real issue here.

"It's so beautiful," said Laurel, totally in awe.

"It's okay."

"Page, it's the most wonderful place I've ever seen."

Laurel crouched in the cool dirt. Rows of grapes started at her feet, then went up and down the hills like slender, well-organized soldiers. Each vine was tied to a stake and when the wind blew, the gangly plants didn't even try to get free.

Laurel let her hair sweep across her face. She breathed the smells into every pore of her body. Damp dirt. Sweet, mashed fruit. A leafy green smell and the residue of some kind of machine oil. Smells that Laurel had not experienced in San Jose, at least not in that combination.

"What's that?" she asked, looking in the opposite direction, across a narrow dirt road. No grapes that way. A fence, tall trees, and a cat tramping through the brush. Farther off was a mobile home with a concrete slab porch. The porch lights flickered on, illuminating a motorbike and an old pickup. Even farther was the road leading to Page's house and the highway.

Page stared down at the highway, waiting for the inevitable caravan of yellow Redwood buses. She barely seemed to see the trailer. "Oh, that's where some people who work on the vineyard live."

"Oh." Laurel rubbed her bare arms. She was shivering. "You're so lucky to live here."

"You think so?"

Laurel nodded. She knew how worried Page was that the kids would hate her when they saw this place. And Page was equally worried that the kids who didn't hate her would treat her like some untouchable millionairess from *Dallas* or *Falcon Crest*. Page's fears were not unfounded. There was a lot here to be jealous of and impressed by. The Hain house was a three-story brick mansion, complete with pillars and a huge, sweeping driveway. It was a house you'd see in a magazine, not a house to live in. The hayride party was being held in a brand-new tasting room. There were fancy cars and maids and Page's oldest sister, Julianne, who had brought her rich and pretty college friends to watch the proceedings and feel superior.

But Laurel wasn't jealous. Not of a stuffy, over-decorated house or a tasting room designed to lure tourists off the highway. And she certainly wasn't envious of Page's family. What she appreciated were the hills that went on forever and the sound of the wind and the wonderful mixed-together smells. After nearly two months in their sterile apartment downtown, Laurel finally understood why her father had picked this town. She loved the openness and the twisted, staked vines. Even the darkening sky stirred her and gave her hope.

Page was sitting in the dirt, hugging her knees like a little kid. "Was your dad glad you were going to this?"

"Boy, was he. My dad believes in joining things, doing what everybody else does." Page nodded and Laurel felt good that she could talk this way. She had told Page a little about her family. How her mom had moved to southern California with her new boyfriend — a guy Laurel didn't like — and then blamed Laurel for choosing her dad. How her dad was a great cook and loved corny jokes. She'd also told Page how close she and her dad were, even though they were very different.

"Maybe it would be better if we joined in," Page wondered out loud.

"You think that if we joined the other freshmen, high school wouldn't be so weird?"

Page threw back her head, changing her mind. Her earrings glistened. "No. I take it back. I can just imagine what my sisters would say. All they tell me is how worthless freshmen are. I'm sure you noticed how friendly they were to you."

That was true. When Laurel's dad had dropped her off, the older Hain girls had viewed her antique dress and lace-up boots with wrinkled noses and huffy sighs.

"I'd rather not even go near this hayride."

"I know." Laurel began to giggle. "Hey, maybe we should sneak off and hop a freight train." She pulled Page up.

Page bounced to her feet as if she were on springs. "Yeah!"

"Which way should we go?"

They looked at the shadowy rows of grapes, then Page gasped and dug her fingers into Laurel's arm. Her nails were chewed short, but she held on so hard it hurt anyway.

"Look! They're coming."

Bus after bus after bus after bus turned off the highway and chugged up the long private road to the Hain house. Horns honked, foggy and low. It was too dusky and distant for them to make people out, but they could tell by the far-off voices that boys were waving their arms and hanging out the bus windows.

Another voice blended in. This one was low, smoky, and annoyed.

"PAGE!"

Whitney was coming from the house, wobbling toward them in very high heels. She was playing the *Dynasty* part for all it was worth. "Page, what are you doing out here? The buses are here."

"I know."

"What are you wearing?"

Page looked down at herself, as if to make sure

she was wearing anything at all. She had on an old Irish knit sweater — big enough to be her father's — baggy khakis and knee-high rubber boots.

"Page," Whitney complained, totally ignoring Laurel. "This is important. You have not exactly made a great impression on my friends so far. You're lucky I'm giving you another chance. I've told you . . . you blow it freshman year and you will be pegged for all of high school." The wind was mussing her hair so she turned to go back to the house. "Come on."

Page's eyes closed shut. "Whitney, do I have to?"

"Yes! I arranged for you to sit on the sophomore wagon." Whitney suddenly noticed Laurel and shot her a phony smile. "Just Page, Laurel. You understand."

"The sophomore wagon!" Page objected, flapping her arms against her dirty pants and stamping a foot. "If I have to go, don't you think I belong with the freshmen?"

Whitney smirked. "Yes, but I'm your big sister, so I'll ignore the obvious and do you a favor." When Whitney realized that Page still wasn't budging she stuck out her lip and taunted, "Oh, what is it, Pagey-poo? Are we upset?"

Laurel intervened. She couldn't bear to see Page pushed any further. "Go ahead without me, Page," she urged. "I'll be fine."

Page wouldn't leave her.

"It's okay," Laurel pressed. "I'll go down to the buses by myself. Just think how proud my dad will be when I tell him I faced my whole class. On my own."

Whitney was checking her watches. One, two, three, as if each one gave her more important information. "Come on, Page." She was still waiting when a voice even smokier and darker than her own rang out.

"WHITNEY!!!"

Julianne, the oldest Hain sister, was standing farther up on the dirt road. Her hair was lighter than Whitney's and Page's, but she was one hundred and ten percent Hain. "Whitney," Julianne demanded. "The buses are here. Are you going to greet people or not? If you don't get this thing off on the right note, the whole evening could be a disaster." She started toward the house, then turned back with a smirk. "And change those shoes. This is a hayride, not your senior prom."

Whitney's limbs tensed. She raised a fist, then forced her arm down, whipped off her shoes, and stormed back to the house.

"Come with me," Page whispered to Laurel.

Laurel shook her head. "You go ahead. They won't let me sit with them. I'll meet you later. I'll go down to the buses by myself."

"Are you sure?"

"I'll meet you after the hayride."

"Do you promise?"

"I'll meet you at the house. Right afterward."

"All right. You promise?"

"I promise."

"Okay." Finally Page slumped off, her feet dragging, her rubber boots kicking up clouds of dirt.

Laurel waited until Page disappeared. She listened to the shouts and the rumbling of bus engines and the far-off whinny of a horse. She took one step toward the road and the hayride, then she hugged herself, turned around, and headed the other way.

CHAPTER 10

Doug waved his arms. His classmates shouted. He wiggled his hips. They giggled and clapped. The clomp, clomp of the horse's hoofs played the bass for him, and the crunch of the wagon wheels provided the rhythm. Tonight even the fluffy, dark sky and the disappearing vines were playing along for Doug Markannan.

"Yes, Doug-o."

"Rap Master Markannan."

Doug bowed. Instead of a tune on his saxophone, he'd invented something new. Freshman rap. Especially tailored to their dilemma. For the hayride the freshmen had been stuck with the most temperamental horse. But Doug believed in making the best of things, and, as usual, his classmates seemed to be doing the same. They rapped. They threw hay at each other. They hung over the side of the wagon and made a hay-passing machine. So far no one, except maybe John Pryble, who was suffering a major allergy attack, had let things put them in a panic.

> "There was a horse named Nugget and he was slow,
> So they gave him to the freshmen since they were low,
> They put them on the wagon that was falling apart,
> 'Cause they just didn't know, those kids got heart.
> Come on baby, don't give me that line,
> THE CLASS OF '89 IS DOIN' JUST FINE."

Doug held out his arms for the finish. And for balance.

"Hey! Whoa!"

Nugget the horse had picked that moment to lurch to a halt. This was about the hundredth time Nugget had stopped to chew weeds, or whatever it was he kept stopping to do. Bets, who sat on a bale near Doug's knees, groaned. As if to spite the freshmen further, the horse looked back at them, then snorted and kicked up his heels. The Dubroskys screamed, which startled Nugget even more.

"Cool out, Nugget!" Doug cried, almost falling into Bets's lap. Bets caught him. Her freckled hands spread over the "W" and the "D" on his Woodstock T-shirt.

"You okay?" Bets asked.

"Sure," he managed. "Thanks."

Doug laughed and Bets pulled away. "What's funny?" she asked abruptly.

"Funny? Nothing's funny." He folded onto the hay bale next to her. It was surprisingly hard. The smell of damp hay filled his head and made him dizzy.

"Oh." She seemed to lose interest in him, squinting instead at Nugget and the driver. The light was disappearing fast. The clouds were changing places, getting grayer and thicker. "Oh, no. I can't even see them, I mean, the sophomore wagon. It's so far ahead. I hope we get back before it's totally dark and . . . you know."

"No, I don't know," Doug teased. He tried to tickle her. When Bets frowned, he contorted his face and hands in a horror-film imitation of the driver. "We'll be stuck out here with him. Like some horror movie — *Freddie and the Freshmen.*"

"Doug." She slapped his arm. That lopsided Bets smile was gone from her face and she looked worried. Doug didn't want her to be worried. He wanted her the way she was a moment ago — with that lopsided smile and her arms coiled around him.

"I wonder how far ahead Micki and Jason are."

Doug didn't want to think about Micki. When Micki was around, he rarely got to be the center of things. And, as goofy as Micki was, she always wanted to do things that had a purpose, a goal. Doug liked doing things just because he felt like it.

"Do you think they really like each other?"

"Who?"

"Jason and Micki."

"How should I know?"

"He's so old."

Doug wanted to say, *Forget about Micki!* When Bets was around Micki she seemed to put all her attention on their girl friendship, as if she was afraid that clever Micki would race ahead and leave her behind. That didn't make sense to Doug. He would never forget Bets.

"How's the horse?" he asked, trying to get her attention back.

"That guy, that driver guy. He's terrible."

As if to illustrate what Bets was trying to say, "Freddie" the driver made an even more inept attempt to get Nugget moving. He growled something that sounded like "Yeeeaap." He clicked his tongue. He slapped the horse with the reins. He slapped again, so hard that the crack reverberated across the vineyard. Bets flinched. Finally the driver got out and tried tugging on the bit. Maybe Nugget was part mule. He wasn't going anywhere.

The freshman mood was turning from mild panic to cranky fear. They all started whining at once.

"I want to go back."

"I'm cold."

"It's getting dark."

John let out another horrific sneeze, while Alice was telling anyone who would listen how sure she was that it was going to rain. The only ones who didn't seem to mind were Paul and Mary Beth, who had picked just this moment to discover their undying affection for one another and start making out. Doug stared at the couple, until Bets caught him staring and they both looked away.

They sat while the trees rustled harder and the air grew damp. It was really starting to get dark. Flashlight dark. The wind was picking up, swirlin a few raindrops and the strong smells of horse and wood and hay.

"I'm freezing."

"Let's go!"

"Somebody make that horse go."

"Somebody do something!"

Doug was starting to wish that Micki'd joined them after all. She was probably the only one who could get them out of this disaster. But wait a second ... whoa. Maybe this wasn't going to be so bad after all.

Doug inched along the hay bale until his side matched up to Bets's. Even in the pitch-dark he could tell that Bets wasn't afraid of the dark or the cold; she was probably just worrying about Micki and the horse. When she realized that he was inching closer, she moved, too. She obviously couldn't figure out why he was crowding her like that.

Suddenly Doug realized that he didn't know how to do this. He'd been thinking about it since he'd first talked to Bets in eighth grade. That was when they'd stayed after class to look at a cow's eye floating in a jar of formaldehyde — Doug thought it was cool to look at; Bets felt sorry for the cow. But they'd become buddies so quickly, and Micki was always around, and besides Doug wasn't sure how you let a girl know that you felt something else for her. When he felt like doing something, he usually just did it. And yet this something was so baffling, so unknown, so exciting, that for one of the few times in his fourteen years, Doug resorted to being devious.

He cleared his throat. "Where's my saxophone?" he asked Bets in a funny voice, because he knew exactly where it was.

Bets bent over to search.

"Is it over there?" he hinted.

She located the Hefty-wrapped case. It was wedged between two bales, on her other side. She reached over to get it and as she did, Doug reached over, too, laughing as he knocked her shoulder, practically falling into her lap. So far so good.

"Doug," she complained, nudging him away with her shoulder and reaching farther.

He wondered if she knew what he was trying to do.

"It's there. Do you want it?" Bets asked.

He tried to think this through. As much as Doug liked to find his own way for things, the only images he could rely on were from the most hackneyed movies and TV. Suddenly Bets was facing him, looking at him, as if she thought he was acting very strangely and she wanted to make sure he hadn't totally lost his mind. He grabbed her shoulders. Too hard.

"Doug, ouch," Bets said, confused. He had a strand of her hair pinned under his thumb. She yanked it free.

He grabbed her shoulder even harder and threw himself at her, locking his lips onto hers. DONE!

She leaned into him and he was sure that the wagon was moving again. He was breathing hard, which made him embarrassed, except that Bets seemed to be doing it, too, and then she shoved him away again. Boy, she was strong.

"What are you — what are you. . . . Are you crazy?" she gasped, her hands flying up to her mouth.

Doug grinned and leaned back. He'd done it. Maybe he'd done it badly, and maybe Bets would be mad at him for a week or two, but he'd make jokes and play his saxophone and Bets would forgive him. Because that was the thing about Doug. He knew he was a fool sometimes and a madman and a crazy. He just didn't let it bother him.

Up ahead, on the sophomore wagon, Micki was sitting next to Jason. She was so charged up she felt like one of those electricity models they had in science class. The current went round and round, hotter and faster. Meanwhile Jason was talking about the floats.

"It's going to be the best, Mick. Every class is doing their share. I have the highest expectations for the freshmen. I know you've been working on that 'Cage the Cavemen' idea, but I think I may have something even better. I also know that anything you do will be so terrific. . . ."

Micki tried to follow the words, but the truth was that it was hard to keep her concentration. The hayride was almost over and Jason was still sitting next to her, smiling evenly and smelling like spice and spring, his chocolate-brown eyes looking only at her.

"So, Mick, what do you think? Do you like my new idea? Are the freshmen going to come through? Micki . . . Micki. . . ."

Micki managed to snap out of her dream state as Jason gently touched her. "Sure, Jason. Sure."

Jason laughed. "Great. I know you can convince the others." He leaned back into the hay bale and put a stalk of hay between his teeth.

Micki, meanwhile, realized that she hadn't thought about her class for several minutes. She had been too much under Jason's spell, but now she was curious. "Jason, can you see the freshman wagon at all?" She stood up and looked back. It was easy to keep her balance. The junior wagon moved along at a rapid, smooth clip. She gracefully sat back down.

"I'm sure they're fine, Micki," he said, sounding like her father when she got too excited or out of control. The other juniors didn't seem any more concerned. They were clumped in their usual groups, gossiping and flirting, as if they were in the Redwood cafeteria rather than trotting along an open field.

Another thing struck Micki as odd. Even though this was the junior wagon, the crowd was pretty mixed. There were seniors on the junior wagon, like Gus Baldwin, senior football captain, and a few others. There were sophomores on the junior wagon, too, and she'd noticed juniors on the sophomore wagon and juniors on the senior wagon. But other than herself and Page Hain, the Class of '89 was segregated.

"Yeah. I'm sure my class is fine, too," Micki said, even though she wasn't sure at all. She felt guilty about deserting her classmates. But what was she supposed to do when Jason turned those puppy eyes on her and asked if she wouldn't mind sitting on the wagon next to him? Besides, she needed to talk to him about the float, so it was for her class . . . sort of. "We're almost back," Micki heard herself saying. "Look at the decorations on the outside. I sure hope it doesn't rain and ruin all that crepe paper and — "

"We are back, aren't we? Darn." Jason frowned. "Well, have you decided? Will you tell my idea to the others?"

When Micki didn't answer, he sighed and took one of her hands. That's when everything stopped. The talking. The float. The heavy cool air and the chatter and the hay. It all disappeared. Jason suddenly slid his other hand under the back of her hair and pulled her to him. Then it hit her. This was going to be even more wonderful than the entire last week put together. More wonderful than anything that had ever, ever happened to her.

Jason gently pulled her toward him and touched her lips with his. Fast. Light. Once. Micki was not so much aware of Jason's lips as she was the crashing of her heart and softness of his cheek.

Micki was skating on ice, falling through air. She watched his mouth, but in a different way than before. She merely nodded when he started talking again about his plans for the parade and how she had to listen carefully because she and the freshmen were going to appreciate his advice.

CHAPTER 11

It started to rain. Not spotty drops or drizzle or mist. Real rain. Rain so thick that you could barely see through it. Rain that you could swim in, that made you so wet so fast there was no point in running for cover. Rain that must have made everyone on the Redwood hayride huddle and scream.

At least Laurel assumed they were huddling and screaming. She wished she knew for sure. She wished she could see them. Or hear them. But she had no idea where they were. Or where she was, either.

"I'm lost," she moaned, her teeth chattering like those mechanical jaws her dad used to buy her for Halloween. The water was running down her bare arms and onto her glasses, which she held in her hand because there was no point in trying to see clearly. For the first time in her fourteen-and-a-half years she wondered if it was always such a good idea to hide and keep to herself.

"Just walk," she ordered herself. "Any direction. Somewhere. Anywhere. Just go."

She was amazed at how frightened she was. Lightning cut hot white zigzags across the sky, and it terrified her. The grapes rattled and shook. As much as she'd appreciated this open land earlier, she wished now that she were back in the apartment with her dad. She wished she were sitting on her tall stool at that silly breakfast counter. She wished she were anywhere rather than out in this too wet, too dark, boundless who-knew-what.

She kept walking — even though the ground got mushier with each step — praying that she would happen upon the road. She tried to remember landmarks she had passed after parting with Page. But all she could see was water . . . and more water and those endlessly staked vines.

She heard something. Something that didn't fit with the rain and the rustling and the slogging of her boots. It was a mechanical hum, a buzz like a tiny electric saw. She knew that no one could be out here in this storm cutting down brush, and yet when she stopped to listen, she was sure that someone was there doing something.

The buzzing got louder and she saw a light. Not a flashlight but a single, dim headlamp. Then nothing but the even, repetitive rain. And a voice.

"Hey. Is somebody out here?" he shouted. "Hello!"

The motor buzzed again; then she heard the squish of tires on mud. Finally he came out of the dark. A boy straddling a motorbike. Close to her age, he had dark hair so wet it was plastered over his forehead and one cheekbone. He wore an old sweatshirt and cut-offs. His bare legs were blotchy with mud.

"What are you doing out here?" he demanded. "Are you okay?"

Laurel recognized the voice but couldn't place it. She wanted to put her glasses back on, so she could make out his face, but she knew that the rain would still make it hopeless to see. Maybe it was a boy from one of her classes, sent from the hayride to look for her.

"Did Page send you?" she asked.

"Who?"

"Page Hain."

He tipped his head back, held onto the handlebars, and let the rain spill onto his face. "Page Hain." He laughed; one sharp, silent laugh.

"Yes." Laurel noticed that his feet were bare and wondered how he could stand it. She was shivering.

"Oh, yeah," he scoffed. "Page Hain sends for me all the time." He stretched his arms and arched his back, drinking in the rain again as if he were one of those tied-up plants.

He wasn't looking for her, Laurel realized. He was out for the fun of riding in the storm. Then it hit her with a shivery start why he was familiar! It was the boy she'd met the first week of school. Jed. The boy in the shop room. She stepped closer to see if he'd recognize her. "Your name is Jed, right?"

Startled, he met her eyes and walked his scooter closer. Actually, it looked more like a tiny motorcycle or a fattened-up bike. "How did you know that?

"We met at school."

"At school?" He cocked his head. "I don't usually meet people at school."

"The first week."

He laid his motorbike between two rows of vines and came closer. So close that Laurel could see the fuzzy outline of his blue eyes and the water dripping down his cheeks and mouth. She wasn't sure he knew her until his eyes opened a little wider and the corners of his mouth crept up. "Oh, yeah." His voice was easier, and a little embarrassed. "I almost knocked you over."

"You did knock me over. I'm Laurel."

"Laurel."

"Laurel Griffith."

He nodded.

"We meet again."

The rain was starting to let up, which made Laurel even colder. It was as if the icy coldness was just now seeping deep into her skin. "Did you leave the hayride?"

"The hayride?"

"The Redwood Hayride. You're a freshman, too, aren't you?"

"Not really. I mean I am, but I don't think of myself as part of any class."

"Why not?"

"I'm on my own, like I told you before. Not part of any school."

117

"You go there, don't you?"

"I go to Giants' games. I go to the movies. That doesn't mean I'm part of them, does it?"

Every answer Jed gave made Laurel feel like it was some kind of oneupsman contest. Even the way he stood and stared — feet planted in the mud, hands on his waist, eyes pasted on hers — felt like a cocky challenge.

"Well, if you don't like high school," she asked, challenging him back, "why did you come to this hayride?"

"I never said I don't like high school. And I'm not here for the hayride."

Laurel was confused. If he wasn't on the hayride, what was he doing out here? And why were they both standing there getting colder and wetter, instead of hurrying back to join the others? "So why are you here?"

"I live here."

"Where?"

He pointed and Laurel put her glasses back on. Through the streaks on the glass and what was now a soft mist, Laurel could make out the road and past that, some blurry yellow light. It was that trailer home she'd noticed before.

"I live with my uncle," Jed continued, that dare in his voice getting sharper. "He works for Mr. Hain."

"You live in that trailer?" As soon as she said it she wanted to take the words back. She hadn't meant to sound so surprised. She just couldn't put it all together.

"Hard to believe, isn't it?" he shot back. "They live there," he pointed in the direction of the

Hain house, "and poor me, I'm just a hired hand."

"Why? Just because your uncle works here?"

He was barely looking at her now. "That's how kids peg me. Last year somebody wrote 'hired hand' on every single one of my books."

He laughed but Laurel didn't. "I just meant, don't you live with your parents?"

"Guess not. Actually, my father lives somewhere in Europe. At least that's what my mother says. I wouldn't know because I never met him. And my mother probably doesn't really know either because she lived here until two years ago when she moved to L.A. She works in a bank there. But she's going to be a movie star. A famous movie star."

"That's nice."

"Nice?" He shook his head. "You really think it sounds nice?"

"No. Never mind."

"Hey, don't be embarrassed. It's like I told you at school. Kids like to peg each other. And if you don't fit the way they fit, then you don't fit, period. You're no different from anybody else."

"And you are?"

"I am. And that's why I can see it. You. I can tell. Let's see." He closed his eyes and set up the picture with his hands. "You live in a nice little house with 1.4 nice brothers and sisters and nice Mom and Dad and a nice dog named Spot. Am I right?"

Suddenly Laurel wanted to be back with the others. She wanted to be anywhere but here with him. She looked around at the mist and the darkness and the mud. "No, that's not how it is."

"Oh, what did I get wrong? The dog's name is Rover? Dog?"

"No."

"It's a cat, then. A little kitten named Fluff."

"Stop it."

"Morris. Boots."

"No!" She had spent so much time and energy pushing back those tears, and this guy, this punk, was going to be the one to force them out! She held the tears back with all her strength. "For your information, I live in an apartment, not a house," Laurel finally blurted, "and I don't have brothres and sisters or a dog or a cat named anything, and I only live with my father because my parents split up eight months ago!"

The toughness rolled off his face as easily as the rain had. For a moment his lips were slightly parted and his eyes went soft. He turned away, stuffed his hands in his pockets, and looked into the cloudy sky. "I'm sorry."

"You don't sound very sorry," Laurel countered. The harder she tried to hold her tears back now, the harder they pushed and spilled. She could only hope that with the rain and the mist, he might not be able to tell. "Do you always just assume things about people like that?"

"No."

"Oh, really?"

"I was just testing you. I like to test people."

"What a laugh. You were just telling me how everybody at school pegs each other here and how it's so great to be alone." Her tears were strangling her. She took deep, sobby breaths, desperate to express herself. "Well, I think you judge other people more than anyone else around here, and I also think that being all alone isn't as great as you think it is!" She stormed past him. She didn't know where she was going, she just wanted to go.

He followed her. "Where are you going?"

She kept sloshing through the muck, heading anywhere, deeper into the vineyard. She didn't care.

"Don't go." He quickly caught up to her and grabbed her arm. "Wait."

"Why should I?" She wrenched her arm away and looked him in the eyes, strong and straight-forward. The tears ran down her face. But she kept looking back.

They stood in the muddy hollow for a long time. The soft rain continued to fall, and Laurel's legs were splattered and there were flecks of mud on her glasses. Still, she played the don't-look-away game with all her might.

He gave in this time. "I'm sorry. Don't cry."

"I'm not."

"I'm sorry. I didn't want to make you cry."

"I'm not crying."

He sighed. "Come on. I'll take you back."

"Just show me the way. I can make it."

"I want to take you back."

"I can make it."

"You can't even see."

Jed stepped toward her and Laurel flinched. His hand went up. Adrenalin shot through her like lightning. She didn't know what he was going to do and yet she was unable to move. Would he grab her arm again or push her down? Finally he reached up, slowly, carefully, and slid off her glasses. He found a chamois cloth in his pocket, wiped the lenses clean, and handed them back.

"Thank you," Laurel said without thinking about it.

She put her glasses back on. For the first time since the rain had started, she saw sharp definitions of color and line. Jed's eyes were a dark, inky color of blue. Teal-green paint was dotted on his sweatshirt, a color Laurel remembered from the doors in the new tasting room. "Paint," she said for some reason, pointing to the speckles on his sleeve.

"You like to paint," he remembered.

"Yes."

His eyes were soft again. "I'm sorry."

"It's okay."

Together they started walking back to where he'd left his bike.

"So why are you out here?" he asked.

"I guess I didn't want to go on that hayride."

"Why did you even come?"

"My dad wanted me to. Page wanted me to."

"You're a friend of Page Hain's?"

"Yes."

"You don't seem like a friend of Page Hain's."

"What does a friend of Page Hain's seem like?"

He didn't answer. They were back where they'd started. He picked up his bike. It was very quiet now that the rain had let up. Laurel wondered how long she'd been out. Time felt stretched out of shape.

"Aren't you cold?" Laurel finally asked, watching him kick the bike pedal with his bare foot.

"I like the rain. How about you?"

She trembled. "I'm okay."

"Climb on." When she hesitated, he held his hand out to her. "I'd better take you back."

Laurel had never ridden on a motorbike before. It seemed too small for both of them.

"Come on. Somebody's probably worried about you."

She reached out. His fingers wrapped around hers. She wasn't sure if it was the dampness or the cold, but she'd never known a person's hand to be so warm before.

"Just put your feet on those," he said, pointing to two small pedals by the back wheel. He let her hand go as she climbed on behind him. "Hold on to me."

She tentatively touched his waist. It was narrow, hard, warm under the wet gray fleece.

"All the way around." His voice had become almost shy. "Otherwise you'll fall off."

"Oh." Slowly she wound her arms around him.

"When I lean to the side, you just stay with me."

"Okay."

"Don't be scared."

"I'm not."

He pushed his foot down again, and the bike rumbled into motion. Leaning, he turned into the dirt path between the vines. The hum of the motor rose as they picked up speed. Laurel thought they would skid sideways at each corner, but she clung and leaned with him. The bike moved evenly over the fallen branches and the ruts until they hit the road. Soon the lights of the house and the tasting room appeared through the mist. Laurel rested her cheek against Jed's damp back and held on tighter.

CHAPTER 12

The freshmen were the only ones still out. The others had made it back long ago and were probably huddled around a blazing Hain fire, guzzling hot chocolate and pigging out on brownies. Not the Class of '89. They were shivering in the open vineyard, waiting for the driver to return with help. The hay stank. The horse stomped and chewed. John Pryble was no longer the only one sneezing his head off. They were all soaked. Catching pneumonia possibly. And more panicked than Bets had ever seen them.

"Yes, boy, yes. It's okay. I know," she cooed to the horse.

She stood outside the wagon, the hood of her yellow slicker over her head. She patted Nugget's belly with big, sweeping hands, checking his bridle, and talked to him — more effectively than she'd talked to just about anyone in her thirteen-and-seven-eighths years. "I know, boy.

I know he hit you and he's mean and horrible. But it's not your fault." She fed him the last of the sugar candy she'd begged off Alice Dubrosky. Sticky, wet lumps. Nugget licked them off her palm.

"Bets, you want some help?"

"No."

It was Doug, hanging over the side of the wagon, gazing at her again.

"Doug, leave me alone."

He looked hurt. "Why?"

"Because. Just . . . because." Of all things Bets was unable to explain, this was the most compicated. What was she supposed to say? Why did you kiss me? After all this time? Does that mean we're boyfriend and girlfriend now? If we are boyfriend and girlfriend, then what? Do we go out on dates? Kiss some more?

The whole thing baffled Bets. When Doug had kissed her, she'd wanted to say, *Don't you dare get lechy and gropey in front of all my friends*. But then that feeling took over. That fainting feeling, as though she had just stepped onto a twentieth-story balcony and someone had taken the floor away. The weirdest part was that Bets had liked that feeling, even though it had terrified her. The only way that Bets could deal with this was to pretend that it had never happened and hope that it would go away.

Oh, why had Micki chosen this evening to desert her! Bets needed Micki to tell her what to do — about Doug, that feeling, the wagon, and her fellow freshmen, who had been left drenched and deserted. Bets always felt as if she was one

126

step behind everything, as though if she'd only had one more year of middle school maybe she'd catch up to Micki and the others. And now she felt even more bewildered and left behind.

"Come on, Nugget. I bet if I drive, you'll take us back, won't you. I won't hit you like he did. Yes."

Just as Nugget seemed to be getting calmer, there was a loud, splatty saxophone bleat. Nugget snorted and bucked.

"Doug, don't," Bets pleaded.

Doug was standing next to her. "It's just me."

"I know."

He lowered his horn, tapping out moisture while Bets went back to soothing Nugget.

"Maybe we should all get out and walk," Doug suggested. "Who knows when Freddie the driver will get back. It's not that far."

Bets inched away from him and peered down the road. The drizzle was light and steady. They couldn't see the Hain house, but maybe it wasn't that far. Walking might have been better than staying there getting waterlogged and hopelessly sick.

"I don't know." Bets stroked Nugget's nose. Maybe walking was the solution. But how was she supposed to get everybody out of the wagon? And what if one or two kids refused to go? "Maybe people won't want to."

"I could play and lead everybody! Sort of like the Pied Piper."

"I don't know."

"Yeah. That's it!"

"Doug."

He was already climbing back onto the wagon and he had that I'm-going-to-do-this-no-matter-what look — the same look he'd had when he'd grabbed her and kissed her. Bets covered her face with her hands and cringed.

Doug's saxophone wailed. Immediately, Bets clutched the reins, expecting Nugget to buck again or run. But Nugget didn't buck. He didn't run or shy or snort. Instead he seemed to ease as the music picked up rhythm and pace.

Bets carefully climbed up, too. She perched on the driver's platform. Flicking the reins, she said, "Giddeup," the way her grandfather used to. She held on tight, and Nugget walked. Out of the weeds, onto the road, and straight ahead. Clip. Clomp. Clip. Even and steady. Bets started to smile.

"We're moving," said John.

"We're saved!" cried Alice.

"Way to go, Bets!"

Everyone applauded. Doug played more loudly and a few kids started to sing.

Bets was afraid that the noise would startle Nugget, but the horse seemed at ease now that she was holding the reins. He ambled happily, only shying once — when they approached the rescue party heading toward them from the house. Bets saw Freddie the driver and another driver on horseback, and behind them a group from Redwood. Mr. Kane and Mrs. Lucht and sophomore Meg McCall with dreamy Nick Rhodes and another couple and a red-headed boy. And Micki! But Bets was having too good a time now to pull in the reins.

"Hi." She grinned as she prodded Nugget into a trot.

Doug played harder. The freshmen launched into "Singin' in the Rain." Even Nugget was stirred by the music, because when Bets tugged again, he went into an even canter, passing the rescue party, and heading back to the house.

Inside the Hain tasting room, the fire crackled. It was crowded and there were portable heating units hanging from the ceiling. Still, it felt cold. The floors were bare wood. The walls were plasterboard marked with white X's and dots. Only the teal-green doors, which were off their hinges and drying in one corner, seemed finished.

"You finally got rid of her," football captain Gus Baldwin told Jason Sandy between downing hot cider and scarfing another handful of cookies.

"Who?"

"Michelle. Micki. That freshman who's been following you around."

Jason took the last cookie out of Gus's hand and popped it into his own mouth. "She's okay."

"Sure. Any girl who has the hots for you is okay." Gus chortled.

"Shut up, Baldwin." Jason wished, just for that moment, that he was an overbulked bully like Gus. He would have mashed Gus's face in. That was about the only thing Gus understood. Force. And food. Gus certainly didn't appreciate the ingenuity and craftiness with which Jason approached life.

Gus burped. "Look." He and Jason were standing in the corner under one of the heating units.

Most of the kids were dancing to Jake and the Twotimers, a local country band hired by Whitney's father. "Look at Hain. You'd think she was Princess What's-her-name, the way she flits around here."

Jason looked. Whitney *was* playing the overgracious hostess. And every phony step she took, she dragged perfect Page along with her. That was the thing about freshmen. They let themselves be dragged along. Just like Micki. Jason thought Micki was quick and sexy and had about enough energy to heat the North Pole. But she was so easy. All it had taken was one kiss and there she was, gaga, in the palm of his hand. Jason got bored by things that came easily. The harder things were, the more he wanted them.

"You guys ever going to win a game this season?" he asked, goading Gus on purpose. "Or are we going to continue this replay of last year, just like I said we would?"

"Don't blame me. At least I didn't get myself kicked off the team."

Jason bristled. "I'm not kicked off."

"Well, benched then. Benched for one game."

Jason had no comeback for that one. He did have to sit out the next game. He'd gone overboard that Friday, instigating a new cheer called the "log roll," where the crowd rolled somebody — preferably a great-looking girl — down the bleachers and onto the field. Jason had seen it work like gangbusters at Napa High. He just hadn't worked the bugs out yet. And he'd made the mistake of picking Hilda Levi. She'd gotten so hysterical that the crowd dropped her and broke her foot. But it was cool. Even though the principal had benched him for the next game, he'd figure that log roll thing out and try it again.

That was another thing that Gus didn't understand. How much Jason wanted that crowd to cheer with him and how far he was willing to go. That was about the only time Jason really felt alive, when that crowd sent the energy racing through his compact body like a toy train on a tight track.

"So who's going to lead the cheers next game?" prodded Gus. "Whitney the Pain?"

"Don't be a moron."

"Good move, Sandy. It's almost homecoming and you get yourself benched. And you call me a moron."

Gus had pinpointed the problem. One game between now and homecoming, and with a losing team and spirit at an all-time low, Jason was sidelined. It was really going to be tough, and that was why Jason wanted it so badly he would do anything for it.

It was all coming down to the homecoming parade. That was Jason's only hope. If he couldn't save the spirit for the school — and for himself — he could at least win that parade contest for his own class.

That was where Micki fit in. Jason had figured the whole thing out. The sophomores were putting a lot of time into their float this year, hoping to win that haunted house contest. Even the seniors were into it. And with football season down the tubes, Jason wanted that parade glory and that contest win more than anything. And the freshmen were going to give it to him. The idea had popped into his brain last night, when he was supposed to be listening to Mr. Tomasino's lecture about Hilda's foot and Jason's responsibility. That was when Jason had figured out that all he had to do was arrange for the freshman float to point up the lawn-chair brigade, to be a complement, an opening act that got the audience warmed up for the real thing. If he could get Micki to provide that for him, he'd have it made.

Jason didn't mention his scheme to Gus. First of all, Gus probably wouldn't understand it. Secondly, Gus hated freshmen and would grab any excuse to bully them — last year Gus had taped a freshman to the flagpole. Thirdly, Jason had already decided to make that farmhouse into a junior lounge, and since Gus was senior, he might not be too keen on the whole idea.

"Hey, what's going on?" Gus grunted, craning his neck and breaking into Jason's thoughts.

"Huh?"

"At the door. Look over there. What's going on?"

Kids were gathering at the front door, peering out, pointing, and laughing. Jason could hear a few voices even over the band.

"I don't believe it."

"They're soaked!"

"Will you look at them?"

Suddenly the band stopped playing. Jason's head buzzed from the sudden quiet. Gus pushed past Jason to check things out, and Jason followed in his wake.

"What *is* going on?" Jason mumbled, half to himself.

The sound of a saxophone and some very silly singing replaced Jake and the Twotimers. Jason had a faint hope that the commotion involved Meg McCall, the sophomore who'd dragged away Nick Rhodes and her other buddies to help look for the freshmen. Now, Meg was hard to get, and consequently Jason had his eye on her. He lifted someone's sweater off a bench, hoping he could catch Meg just as she straggled in and be the one to bundle her up.

But Jason didn't see Meg or Nick, or their buddies Allie or L.P. or Sean. He didn't see the teachers who'd gone out, or the drivers, either. What he saw, and heard, was a wagonful of idiotic freshmen, dancing and sneezing and singing. They were led by the dopey guy with the saxophone around his neck. He was acting more outrageous than any of them, bobbing up and down with his saxophone as if he thought he was a guest rocker on *Saturday Night Live*.

"I hate freshmen," growled Gus.

Jason nodded as he watched the underclassmen climb down from the wagon. He knew what Gus meant. He didn't like it when freshmen were too easy, but he didn't like it when they didn't know their place, either.

Page panicked when she realized that Laurel wasn't on the freshman wagon. Painful panic. True fear that someone she really cared about, her first high school friend, might be in trouble.

"I should never have left Laurel out there," she told herself. "Never, ever, ever." She was standing behind Whitney, listening to her gossip with a group of senior girls. So far they had put down the looks or the clothes of almost every other girl in the tasting room, including Whitney's closest friends. Page couldn't stand it anymore. She started to walk away.

"Page, where are you going?" Whitney demanded.

Page was heading for the back room. There were rain jackets back there and boots and hats that the workmen wore. She was going to suit up, go out in the storm, and search for Laurel.

Whitney followed her into what would eventually become the tasting room kitchen. Now it was just a big room with a skylight and vents and plumbing outlets waiting to be hooked up. In the corner was a refrigerator in a giant cardboard box. The air was heavy with sawdust and damp paint. Page went right for the stack of work clothes, grabbed a pair of coveralls, and climbed into them.

Whitney looked appalled. "Have you lost your mind?"

Page ignored her. She'd been pushed and prodded and pointed at enough for one night.

"PAGE! I'm talking to you. What do you think you're doing?"

For once Page wasn't concerned with her sister or the anger building inside her. She had something much more important to attend to. She had to find Laurel.

Page grabbed a stocking cap and opened the

back door. But what she saw startled her. Laurel. Laurel was no more than twenty feet away. Standing as calmly and easily as if she'd been there all night. And next to Laurel was Jed Walker, the boy who helped his uncle pick grapes and paint fences and move irrigation pipe. Page had never talked to him. She wasn't supposed to. But Laurel was standing next to his motorbike, and she was talking to Jed. They were both spattered with mud.

Before Page could stop her, Whitney was in the doorway, too.

"Oh, great." Whitney swore. "Perfect. What in the world is she doing with him? Maybe he'll come in and start a fight like he did last year at Portola. I warned you about her, Page. I warned you."

"Laurel!" Page called.

Jed looked over first. Instantly he pulled way from Laurel and started his bike. The motor stalled and he tried again. Laurel took a few steps toward Page.

"Where were you? Have you been out here the whole time?" Page asked.

Laurel was shivering, but her face looked oddly dreamy and peaceful. "I got lost."

"I was so worried."

"Jed gave me a ride back."

Page glanced back at Whitney, praying that for once her sister would keep her nasty mouth shut. But Whitney merely grimaced and stared. Then there was a loud *vvrroomm* and a wild cloud of dirt. Page looked back into the night. Jed and his motorbike were gone.

CHAPTER 13

By Monday morning the sun had come out again. It shone down through a hazy sky and sparkled off the duck pond in Portola Park, as well as the signs in front of the Albertson's that advertised that week's special: jugs of fresh apple cider, almonds and walnuts, jumbo-sized pumpkins.

In spite of the cheerful displays, neither Micki nor her brother Peter said anything for a while as his Volkswagen rumbled along. He'd just spent another weekend at home discussing "life" with their parents, and even though Micki needed advice, she wondered if he was talked out.

He cut across two lanes of traffic, pulling into the parking lot of the Big Bear minimall. Then he turned off the engine and looked at Micki with warm, inquisitive eyes. "Are things okay with you? I never get to talk to you anymore."

"Sure."

Peter leaped over for what he called a "kamakazi tickle" then swung back to open the car door. "I don't believe you. We will continue this discussion as soon as I get fuel for my magnificent body."

They both smiled and then Peter was running across the parking lot. Micki watched him jog into a Winchell's Donut shop and, in spite of all the teasing, she marveled at how graceful he was. Even after several weekends of worrying her parents, he still looked like the confident, directed Peter she'd always admired. She could never imagine Peter losing his entire sense of sanity over one kiss — even if it was his first — delivered on a bale of moldy hay from someone he had an agonizing and possibly hopeless crush on.

He was already back, tapping on her window. "Catch." Peter tossed in a white paper sack and raced around to the other side.

Micki opened the bag as he slid in. The smell of sticky, sweet frosting overwhelmed her. "These are brownies, Peter."

"I know," he said, fishing one out as he started the car again. "I didn't have any breakfast."

Micki wrinkled her nose. "That's your breakfast? Gross."

"Hey, I'm loading carbos." He stuffed the brownie into his mouth and grinned. "I know, Mick. I know you think I'm perfect. And you think you have to be perfect, too. That's the way our parents raised us. But I'm finally figuring out that it just doesn't work that way." With that he set the other brownie on his lap.

Micki picked off a few nuts and some specks

of chocolate. "I'm hardly perfect," she said, trying not to flinch from the sweetness. Peter maneuvered behind the traffic backed up for Redwood High. A big bus spewed smoke ahead of them, and three kids on bikes sped by to take shortcuts onto campus.

"I know," he agreed. "You just think you should be. So tell me what's bothering you. I sort of dominated the parent sympathy this weekend. . . ."

"No, you didn't."

"Micki." He nudged her. "I did. So, what I want to know is, what could possibly be getting my wonderful, funny, very special sister down."

"I'm not special."

"Are you arguing with me?"

For once, Micki couldn't explain herself. Her last two days had been a combination of thrilling rushes, terrifying curves, and painful spills — like when she and Bets used to speed down curvy Capitola Mountain on their skateboards. First Jason had asked her to join him on the bus and the wagon. Then he'd kissed her. Then he'd seemed preoccupied for the rest of the evening. Then yesterday, when she was convinced that this whole romance was some sort of joke, he called to see how she was and to talk some more about the freshman float. Micki's heart felt like a battered pinball.

"There's this guy."

"Aha! I knew it."

"Peter! He's a junior." She buried her face in her hands. "Do you remember what it's like to be a freshman?"

"I will never forget."

Suddenly Micki flashed on Peter when he'd started at old Sonoma High. The picture that popped into her head was from his freshman yearbook. Peter hadn't been handsome then. His ears had stuck out and his nose looked too big. She wondered if his ears and nose had since shrunk, or if the rest of him had grown.

"So what about this guy?"

"Well, it's kind of involved. This whole homecoming thing is coming up, the week after this. The parade and the game and the dance are a week from this Friday."

Peter grinned. "Ah, homecoming. I can see you need some serious brotherly advice."

Instead of following the traffic and turning onto campus, he sped a block ahead and parked across from the baseball diamond and the soccer field. Micki turned around to watch the school buses chug into the Redwood lot.

"Peter, maybe you'd better take me to the parking lot. I usually meet my friends there, and my first-period class is on that side. I might be tardy."

Peter plucked the key out of the ignition and faced her. "Mick, talk to me and let your friends wait. And you can be late to class for once in your life. Believe me, I used to do it all the time."

"You did?"

"Another thing you didn't know about me. See, I'm not as perfect as you thought." He crumpled his empty doughnut bag and tossed it in the backseat. "See, I'm a slob, too. So tell me more about homecoming and . . . THIS BOY!"

"Okay."

She explained and Peter listened. She told him how wacko she got whenever Jason was near her, but now she wasn't sure how he felt. It made her crazy because one moment she'd be flying, and the next she'd have crashed to the floor. What did Peter think about Jason's suggesting a new design for her float — "Sit on the Cavemen," as opposed to Micki's "Cage the Cavemen" idea? Jason said that his idea of a grizzly bear sitting down in a lawn chair, to tie in with the juniors' marching brigade, would be much funnier, and have a much better chance of winning the Haunted House contest. He'd gone on and on about it over the phone. Her friends had already put a lot of work into "Cage the Cavemen," but Micki knew that if she really pushed it, they'd change the theme. But what did Peter think?

"I think it means that this guy is as pathetic as I was when I was in high school," Peter said.

"He's not."

Peter laughed. "Gee, thanks. I just mean I remember calling girls I liked and going on and on about the dumbest things — like homecoming floats — because I couldn't think of anything else to say."

"So you think he likes me?"

"How could anybody not like you?"

Micki poked his stomach then reeled back. She suddenly felt light as helium. "You bozo."

"Well, now that we're back on a high plane, I guess I'll take you to school." Peter swung a wide, illegal U turn, and swerved over to the main Redwood entrance.

"It all sounds really stupid to you, doesn't it?" Micki sighed. "I think I'm just getting crazy because of all the pressure with this homecoming float. What does it really matter, right? I'm just making a big deal out of something completely dumb."

"Now wait a minute," Peter objected. "Let's not refer to one of the high points of my life as completely dumb. Let us remember that you are looking at the now-defunct Sonoma High's final homecoming king."

Micki frowned.

"What, Mick?"

"Oh, nothing. I forgot about the princess thing." Peter shot her a look of disbelief. "For the last ten minutes, that is." She scanned the parking lot as Peter drove up to the loading strip. The preliminary princess elections were coming up that Wednesday. Five nominees from each class would be selected and announced at Friday's football game, with another election for the final winners the following week. All the freshman gossip pointed to Page Hain. The idea of Page winning princess was so painful that Micki couldn't think about it without getting a hot lump in her throat.

"You planning to go to the homecoming dance, Mick?"

Of course she hoped — had actually gotten down on her knees and prayed — that Jason would ask her. But she didn't mention that to Peter. She knew she didn't have to. "I don't know."

"I could come home again and be your date, if you get really desperate."

Micki laughed. "Even I'm not that desperate."

"Nah. I guess not."

Micki's friends were waiting for her at the bottom of the side stairs. Right away Doug started yelling about choosing a float headquarters, and Bets and the twins were gesturing something about spray paint, and pretty soon the whole gang was jumping up and down and waving for Micki to hurry up and join them. "I guess I'd better go."

"Your public is waiting."

" 'Bye."

He gave her one last smile before driving away.

"I'm sick of homecoming," Doug said to himself that afternoon. "And it won't even be here for two more weeks."

He was walking across the parking lot, tapping out a new band tune on his thigh. It was almost four o'clock and practice was over. Everybody was talking about homecoming . . . theme dressing days, the parade, the dance, the game. All his friends were over in the theater-to-be, starting work on the float. He was supposed to be there, too, but somehow he just wasn't in the mood.

At first he thought he was just annoyed because they'd all voted to change the float idea at lunchtime. When he thought about it, "Sit on the Cavemen" wasn't all that different from "Cage the Cavemen," and in either case they could use their skills and make a terrific float and maybe even win the contest. And yet something about changing the theme just didn't feel right. He didn't know why, but it didn't.

Then Doug passed the bike rack and saw Bets's blue Schwinn with its big metal basket. Instantly he recognized another reason he didn't feel like going over to work on the float. Bets. Bets had been acting cool and unnatural to him all day. Since the hayride, actually, when he'd kissed her. He wondered if it was always a good idea to do exactly as he pleased. Maybe he should think about things like kissing girls before he did them.

Doug slouched against the bike rack and sank slowly to the ground. He groaned aloud and picked at the sparse grass. "Who am I supposed to talk about this with?"

The weirdest part of all was that the one person Doug could imagine talking about all those things with (not just the funny stuff) was Bets. Even though he'd never talked seriously with Bets before, and even if she might not be able to express herself in return, he still had the feeling that she would understand. If only he hadn't screwed things up. "Dumb," Doug said.

Just then he saw Bets come down the side stairs and amble across the lot. He watched her carefree walk and the way she scuffed her cowboy boots along the asphalt as if she were dancing. He knew the best thing for him to do was ignore her, or even better, leave before she spotted him. But before he could think about it he was on his feet, waving, with his voice booming halfway across Redwood Hills.

"BETS!"

When she saw him, her gait turned stiff. She

approached her bike and unlocked it as if he weren't there.

Doug stood very still. "Hi."

"Hi." She said it in that clipped way that was really starting to get to him.

"How's the float going?"

She shrugged and refused to answer.

Doug wanted to shake her — and himself. Regardless of how much he'd enjoyed that kiss, nothing was worth ruining their friendship. Nothing.

"Bets, can I talk to you?"

"Isn't that what you're doing?" She swatted up the kickstand on her bike, then hiked it out of the rack.

When she started to walk away, Doug stopped her. "Don't worry. I'm not going to attack you again."

"I — I didn't say you were," she stammered.

"Bets!" Now that he had her attention, he wasn't quite sure what it was he needed to say. How exactly do you feel about me? . . . Do you take me seriously? . . . Do you think you'll ever take me seriously? . . . Do you think anyone will ever take me seriously?

"Well, uh, well, see. . . ."

"What, Doug?"

Great. He sounded like her. "Bets, do you think I'm too much of a clown?"

For the first time she almost looked at him. Her face filled with sympathy. "No. I don't think. . . . Well, Doug, you're . . . funny and. . . ."

What was he doing? Trying to get Bets to tell him that he was a fabulous charmer, to bolster

144

him the way she did Micki? Doug realized she would do it out of sheer sweetness, if she thought that was what he needed to hear. But he'd rather really be a clown than someone who needed to be flattered and lied to.

"Forget that. Rewind. That wasn't what I wanted to say at all," Doug protested.

"What?"

"Never mind."

"Doug!"

He drew a deep breath. For some reason looking at her now made him feel more for her than when they were sitting in the dark on the wagon. His voice choked up.

"I just wanted to say that I . . . I thought you did a great job bringing the freshman wagon in after the hayride."

"You did?" Her eyes softened.

"Yes!"

She stood a little taller. "I did, didn't I!"

He was surprised by her spark of confidence. She had a gleem in her eye that made him want to be just as forthright. "And mainly I want to say that I hope we're still friends. Because I like being friends with you and I hope I didn't blow it. That's all."

"That's all?"

Doug nodded and felt himself cringing as if Bets was about to deliver a punch to his midriff. She picked up the handles of her bike and started walking it, instead.

"Okay," she said.

He jogged after her. "That's all you can say? Okay? I bare my soul to you and you say okay?"

"What am I supposed to say?"

"How about: Doug, you're funnier than Steve Martin, more talented than Michael Jackson, and handsomer than Rob Lowe?"

Her mouth twisted in that lopsided grin. "How about: You're not as bad as Freddie."

"I'll accept that."

"Good." She slugged him.

"Ow!"

"Serves you right."

"For what?"

"You know for what." She hopped on the bike, balancing her weight on one pedal, and gliding along standing up. "I have to go get food for everybody. Come and help me."

"Well, I don't know if I — "

"Everybody's starving, Doug. Why do I always do this stuff by myself? Come on."

"Pushy, pushy."

"Doug."

"I'm coming. Okay, I'm coming."

"Well, hurry up!" She swung her leg over the seat and took off as if she were entering the Grand Prix.

CHAPTER 14

It was like standing under a basket of people. Or looking up through a grate in the street. Laurel and Page saw shoe bottoms — complete with squashed jelly beans and sticky candy wrappers — Redwood athletic programs and coats and books and Thermoses and empty cups. It was dark and slightly damp. Things fell on their heads.

"I wonder how many freshmen have seen a football game from under the bleachers before," said Laurel.

Page poked her. "Who can see?"

Laurel stood on her tiptoes and attempted to peer out. As she did, the crowd started to roar. "Wait, I think something's happening. Yes. Guys are running and jumping on each other." The cheering swelled. "Oh, no, here it comes again. Cover your ears!" The people above them started stamping their feet. It was the last game before homecoming week and the crowd was so wild it sounded like the stadium was being blown up.

"EEEEE!" they both yelled, holding their heads and stamping, too. The cheering weakened.

"Did we score?" Page tugged on Laurel's sweater and yelled, "Laurel, are we winning?"

"I don't know," Laurel giggled. "I don't understand football."

The referee whistled and the crowd groaned. The stamping was replaced by rustling: kids sitting back down and rearranging lap blankets. Page and Laurel roamed and kicked gravel with their feet. They were under the student bleachers, exploring their territory as if it were someplace noteworthy and unique.

"What if Whitney catches you under here?" Laurel asked. They were only at the game because Whitney had insisted Page attend. And because Laurel's father had begged her to do the same.

"Somehow I don't think this is one of Whitney's hangouts."

Laurel glanced around at the puddles and the trash. "I guess not. But, you know, I think it has possibilities."

Page posed with her nose in the air. "I'm sure my mom's decorator could do wonders with it." They giggled. "How do you find these places?"

Even Laurel had to admit that this was one of the best hideouts at Redwood. "Talent." Laurel leaped upward and swung from a metal pipe that went from the ground to the very top bleacher. That's when the band, who was sitting in the corner just above them, launched into "Rock Around the Clock."

"Shall we?"

"Why not?"

They danced until the band stopped playing, and the crowd started to applaud and cheer again.

Laurel and Page applauded, too.

Page ducked over to the side to see what was going on. "The second quarter must have started," she worried, peeking out through the wall of wire mesh. The area under the bleachers was fenced. They'd only been able to sneak in because someone had left the back gate unlocked.

"What does that mean?"

"It's half way to halftime."

"Oh."

They both knew what that meant. Halftime was when the princess nominees from each class were being announced. Each nominee would have to go down to the field and take a bow.

"I guess you'd better sneak back out pretty soon," Laurel admitted. "It might look a little weird to have a freshman nominee crawl out from under the first row."

"You think so?"

"It might attract attention."

"It might." Both girls lingered around the pole. Finally they sat together on a lumpy mound of concrete. "I could just stay here."

"I think your sister would miss you."

"You have a point." Page closed her eyes and chanted, *"Please don't let me get it. Please don't let me get it. Please, please, please don't let me get it."*

"Forget it, Page," Laurel sympathized. "Your fate is sealed."

"UGH!"

Laurel listened to the crowd while Page prayed that the rumors, the gossip, even the guaranteed-authentic-inside-dope that Whitney had discovered, were all untrue. The election on Wednesday had been a write-in — the freshmen could nominate any five girls in their class. Kids had already told Page that they'd put her name down. But the worst evidence was Whitney's inside info, which she'd manipulated out of Roger Sandler, head of the homecoming committee. Roger, who had the hots for Whitney, leaked that Page had received more votes than any other two frosh girls put together. If the preliminary vote was any indication, Page would probably win the final election as well.

Of course, Whitney had delivered this news to Page with some added opinions of her own . . . like that this was a chance for Page to finally make her mark . . . and that Page had better not blow it this time . . . and that Page must be incredibly lucky, because Whitney couldn't see what she'd done to deserve it. That was one of Whitney's few opinions that Page agreed with.

"I don't deserve it," Page told Laurel.

"What?"

"Winning. That is, if Whitney was right about the voting. Why should I even be nominated? I haven't done anything."

Laurel kicked aside somebody's old glove. It was stiff with dried mud and had probably been there since last year. "Don't be upset, Page. It's not so bad. They could be electing you as creep of the year or something."

"I'd like that better."

"Page, don't."

Page's face had started to redden. "Don't you see, Laurel? If I win it will just be one more reason for everyone to hate me. Even the people who voted for me, they just did it because they think I'm some kind of big deal. But they'll find out that I'm not. And then they'll hate me even more!"

Laurel put an arm around her, holding her tight until Page began to relax. "You could drop out," she suggested finally. "If you really want to, that is. On Monday, before the final vote, you could withdraw."

Page plopped her head onto Laurel's shoulder. She hadn't thought of withdrawing, and it actually seemed like a good idea. She wanted to ask Laurel if she thought the rules allowed her to drop out, but she couldn't because there was a burst of mayhem overhead. The crowd was on another stamping rampage. The cheerleaders were screaming, and someone was pounding on a bass drum.

Page and Laurel rushed up front to find out what had happened. They couldn't see a thing, so Laurel led the way to the back gate instead. The view back there was the opposite of the lights and the pom-poms and the dirt-stained uniforms. They saw parents carting refreshments, three New Wave kids, and a gang that looked like middle-schoolers. Beyond that was the open field bordered by the street, lit only by the spill from the streetlamps, but Laurel could make out a little kid doing wheelies on a bicycle, two girls sharing a cigarette, and a boy walking a motorbike. She stared harder. Everything inside her stopped, reversed, picked up speed. The boy with the motorbike looked like Jed.

Laurel's fingers curled around the wire fence. She felt as if she were being lifted, as if a giant had stepped behind her and hauled her up by the collar. She told herself it wasn't Jed. She'd looked for Jed all week at school, even taken Page on two unexplained lunchtime hikes to try and find him. She'd discovered chess nerds and drama freaks, heavy metal kids and fieldies. She'd even gone back out to industrial arts. She'd found new hiding places. But she hadn't found Jed. She'd almost come to the conclusion that he never went to school at all.

"What is it? What are you looking at?" Page asked.

"Nothing. No one." Laurel was afraid he would turn around and really be a sophomore or someone from Petaluma High. Someone. Anyone but Jed.

Page suddenly saw him, too. "Isn't that Jed Walker?" she blurted.

Laurel didn't answer. She still wasn't sure. And Jed was the one issue that she and Page had only discussed once since the hayride. Page had told her about a fight Jed was supposedly in at Portola. Page remembered hearing that Jed was suspended for a few days. Other than that, he was just a "hired hand." Page and Jed were two parts of Laurel's new life that didn't fit together.

"What's he doing out there?" Page pressed into the gate to get a better look. "Did he drive that bike all the way down here?"

A car slowed as it passed the school, spraying hot light over the bike and the boy. Laurel saw his dark hair, his denim jacket, the defensive way he stood, and then, his face. It was Jed, all right.

"What is it? What are you looking at?" Laurel asked.

"I'm sure he's not allowed to ride that bike off the vineyard," Page snapped.

"That's probably true," Laurel shot back. "But I'm sure we're not supposed to be under these bleachers, either."

Page was quiet. She stared out while the crowd overhead chanted "GO, GO, GO, GO!" over and over.

"I'm sorry," Laurel whispered.

"It's okay," Page sighed. "Laurel, he just seems so. . . ."

"So different from us."

"I guess."

"He's not."

They slipped through the gate, carefully closing it behind them. No one noticed them. People were hurrying by, carrying paper cups and steamy hot dogs. A middle school boy stumbled, scattering an armload of candy. Laurel didn't see him. She was gazing out at the field.

"Do you want to, I don't know, go say hello to him?" Page whispered.

Laurel wasn't sure why, but she knew that she had to talk to him. To see him one more time at least. She usually hid and waited, but this time she felt like her legs had already run across that field. There was no choice to be made. She nodded.

"Will you come back?" Page asked, a little panicked.

Laurel turned to her, as if she'd just remembered that Page was still there. "Yes. Of course. I could just go see him for a minute, couldn't I? I . . . I never got to thank him for giving me a ride back that night."

An enormous cheer erupted, and the entire Redwood student section rose to its feet. The people heading back from the refreshment stand hugged their goodies to their chests and ran. Page and Laurel didn't budge.

"Will you be okay without me?" Laurel asked.

"I just have to walk down on the field when they call my name. Then Whitney will know I'm here."

"I'll be right back." Laurel stared out across the field again. "Where should we meet?"

Page noticed the drill team and the flag twirlers lining up near the refreshment stand. "Let's pick a place to meet away from here. Just in case we can't find each other."

Laurel agreed. "At your locker. As soon as halftime's over, if I don't find you before."

"Okay."

"I'll be at your locker at the end of halftime." Laurel started to run, then turned back. "Are you sure you'll be all right?"

Page turned to smile. "I'll just make sure that no one notices me, go on the field really fast, and then leave." She cringed as Whitney's hoarse voice led the crowd in an even louder yell.

"Are you positive?"

Jed was walking his bike toward the street. "You'd better go," Page urged. "He's leaving."

Laurel turned to look and her face fell.

"Go on."

Laurel ran back, flew at Page with a quick hug, then took off across the grass. "I'll meet you later!"

"Later," Page repeated, almost to herself.

The crowd was screaming and stamping again. "We're the Grizzlies, we're the Grizzlies, F-I-G-H-T!" The band joined in, too. Page noticed the lines of drill-team girls and flag twirlers snaking toward her, getting ready for the halftime show. She scooted out of their way and jostled through the crowd until she stood at the edge of the student bleachers.

There was a tuba at the end of one bench and two of those white band hats that Whitney said made the musicians look like marching Q-Tips. The cheerleaders and Whitney were down front, whirling and leaping like pairs of giant scissors. This was the first time Page had been able to see the scoreboard. The Grizzlies were ahead seven to six! Three minutes were left in the second quarter. Page looked vaguely into the stands and tried to figure out where she was going to sit.

That's when she saw Jason Sandy, slumped in the third row, wearing his yell leader uniform. Page wondered why he wasn't on the field and then remembered that he'd been benched because of that stupid log roll stunt. Whitney'd whined about it all week, although Page suspected that her sister was really pleased to have more of the limelight to herself.

"PAGE! HEY, WHERE YA BEEN?" Jason jumped up and hollered.

Page responded with a stiff smile. Jason had come up to her a few times in the last week. She had a funny feeling that his sudden attention was somehow connected with the princess election, yet she didn't see how that could really be. Whitney had sworn that she was the only person, besides Roger Sandler, who knew the inside scoop.

Jason waved her over. "COME SIT WITH ME, PAGE!" It looked like he was all by himself.

Page waffled. She had to sit somewhere, but she didn't quite trust Jason — or like him for that matter. She was considering staying right there on the sidelines, when she heard another voice shout her name.

"Page, there you are!"

It was Natalie Bonwit, Whitney's friend.

"Whitney told us to save you a seat."

Natalie was in the middle of the stands, surrounded by a dozen other overdressed, upper-crust, upperclass friends of her sister's. They were all the girls who made Page feel like nothing. But Natalie kept beckoning and finally Page obeyed. Slowly stepping over the first bench, she began to climb.

And that was when Page saw Micki Greene. As much as she and Micki tried to avoid one another after that awful soccer game, they never seemed to stay totally out of one another's way. There was still the hayride and gym class and chance meetings in the hall or the quad. And those meetings always resulted in the gut-churning stalemate they were in now. No matter what else was bobbing or waving around them, her eyes and Micki's eyes would furiously lock together as if they were on a tractor beam.

"PAGE!" repeated Natalie. "Don't just stand down there like an idiot. Come on up."

Micki was locked onto her. She was just waiting for Page to join Whitney's snotty friends so she could whisper to Betsy Frank how Page was a phony and a snob. And then Betsy would whisper to the next girl who would whisper to the next and the next, until the whispers had spread over the entire stadium. Page could already hear them.

The only thing louder than those whispers was Jason's voice, calling to her again. "COME SIT WITH ME, PAGE!"

Page stepped down. Joining Jason seemed the only solution. Whitney said Jason was on the outs now. Maybe people would think Page was more human if she sat with somebody like that. Or even better, maybe Jason had become a non-person — like Whitney said he had — and she could disappear next to him.

Page unlocked her gaze from Micki's and made her way down to Jason. As she climbed over purses and jackets and piles of empty soda cups, she decided that this was the right thing to do. Sitting with Jason Sandy was probably as safe as she could get.

CHAPTER 15

Everybody around Micki was cheering, but Micki couldn't remember the words. If there was anyone who'd learned all the fight songs, all the Grizzly yells, it was Micki. She was famous for her memory — renowned. She had won the seventh-grade spell-off at Portola. She'd been the first eighth-grader to recite the Gettysburg Address in history class after Mr. Trout had assigned the project. So why was she drawing a blank on words that were nearly as familiar as her own name?

It wasn't because of the nip in the air, or how exciting the game was turning out. Redwood was still ahead by one point. Bets and Micki's other friends were huddled around, sharing blankets and ponchos and passing Styrofoam cups of hot chocolate and cider. They had no problem remembering the yells. They screamed their heads off. Big horse-cheers that made their cheeks glow and their eyes bright. Micki was the only one whose mind had blanked out. She was the only one who felt as if her entire being had just been smothered by a large, plastic tarp.

"BEAR TO THE LEFT, BEAR TO THE RIGHT. . . ."

"C'mon, Mick." Bets was nudging her, and the whole row of freshmen that surrounded Micki began swaying back and forth. White gloves from the Pep Club were coming together in muffled claps. Down below, the cheerleaders were doing a high-step with their pom-poms extended like in a chorus line. Even Doug — over near the end zone with his furry white band hat slipping over his eyes — was cheering.

Micki put her hands together. She forced words out of her mouth, but she felt as if she were on automatic pilot. Then her gaze drifted and her brain scrambled again. They were still there. Jason and Page. Four rows down and twenty bodies over. Jason was laughing . . . whispering into Page's ear. His arm was attached to her shoulder. Micki had that awful feeling again and she shivered, even though she wasn't cold. This feeling was more like hot wind gusting in from the desert.

"GRIZZLIES, GRIZZLIES, GRRRRRR-OOOWWWWL. . . ."

"Drop him, Baldwin."

"Run, Rhodes, run!"

The ball was in play again, though there were only forty seconds on the clock. Another time-out was called, and Micki was amazed that the quarter wasn't over. This had to be the longest three minutes in history. Her eyes were pulled over again. Jason's arm was still attached. He was still whispering. Page leaned in to hear what he was saying, and her mismatched earrings glittered under the lights. Micki had a horrible desire to rip those earrings right off her ears.

"You okay, Mick?" said Bets. "Are you nervous about halftime?"

"About what?"

Bets raised her voice and spoke more slowly. "About princess, I mean. Nervous. Don't be. I know you'll be nominated."

"Me, too," seconded Alice Dubrosky, who sat one row back.

Other freshmen patted Micki and joined in.

"I put your name down."

"So did I."

"You'll get it."

Get what? Micki wanted to yell back at them. Or rather, get who? What did it matter if she was nominated? What did any of it matter now? The election. The float — which she'd worked on like a maniac all week, changing all her designs to fit Jason's ideas. Who cared about any of it if Jason was going to walk off in the middle and fall for ... of all people ... Page Hain!

Everyone screamed when the ball went into play again. The roar from the stands almost blew Micki's eardrums out; and at the same time, she heard nothing. She was thinking. Thinking about how everything was a sham. Freshman year. Jason's kiss. Bets insisting that she was pretty. Peter telling her that she was special. All lies. Pretty and special, kisses and homecoming crowns. Those things were saved for girls like perfect Page Hain.

The Petaluma team ran one last play where Nick Rhodes intercepted the ball and promptly knelt down to eat up the clock. The buzzer went off. There was Grizzly pandemonium. The freshmen were hollering, and some of the girls were riding the guys piggyback while the players trotted off the field. But things calmed down almost right away, and all eyes went back to the fifty-yard line.

Mark Coffield, a Redwood graduate and last year's homecoming king, strode down front. He bowed cornily, then helped the student council members set up a microphone and roll out a ratty red carpet.

Mark stepped up to the mike. "Ladies and gentlemen, I have the honor of announcing the nominees for this year's homecoming court."

Bets grabbed Micki's wrist and squeezed her eyes shut, whispering, "Come on, Micki," over and over.

Micki was amazed by how much Bets wanted her to win, especially since the whole thing suddenly seemed unreal. Then Micki grabbed Bets back as she realized that this was much too real and could become even more grim. She might not even be nominated.

"We'll start with the freshmen." Mark squinted up into the bleachers. "Where are you, freshmen?"

All around Micki there was hooting and pig-snorting. Paul O'Conner threw confetti, and John Pryble tossed down somebody's hat and gloves.

"Ah, yes. There you are." Mark unfolded a sheet of paper. "Okay. We're going to start with the Class of '89. Come down here, ladies, when I call your name." Mark cleared his throat and began. He mispronounced the first two frosh names, Libby Altbaum and Karen Dunere, but there was no confusion because Libby was the sweetest freshman alive, and Karen dated the J.V. quarterback, so they were both obvious choices.

"Michelle Greene" rang out next, and Micki wasn't even sure she'd heard it, because Bets and her other friends were jumping up and hugging her and shoving her toward the aisle.

Micki somehow negotiated the benches and the bodies and made it safely onto the field, only aware of one thing: the next nominee . . . Page Hain. It seemed like the name announced after that was Cindy White's, but it didn't matter because when Micki took her place on the long red carpet, she was standing next to Page. For a split second their eyes locked, until they both looked away and pretended the other didn't exist.

Micki stood there, dizzy from the stadium lights and all the red in the bleachers. The marching band was a block of blue in the end zone, and there seemed to be banners and pom-poms everywhere. As Mark went on to announce the older nominees, only a few names made it through the thick web of Micki's brain. Whitney for the sophomores . . . of course. Meg McCall. Then Mark was announcing that the senior king nominees needn't come down, since some of the guys were on the team and they might have to — ha ha — run out of the locker room naked.

Polite applause signaled the end of the announcements. Micki spacily wandered off the field while the microphone was being taken down, the red carpet rolled up. Doug and the rest of the band were taking over. The flag twirlers and the drill team began their drill. All Micki saw was Page.

Instead of heading back into the bleachers, Page lingered down front with the cheerleaders. Whitney had her arm around Page, and in front of the entire crowd was cheering, "Vote for Page. P-A-G-E! Vote for Page."

Micki couldn't stand it anymore. She ground her feet into the dirt, didn't move when people tried to get by her, didn't climb back up to her seat. Soon Bets was at her side, as well as the twins and Cindy White.

"Congrats," Cindy whispered. She stood behind Micki and watched Page over Micki's shoulder. The band played a medley from *Cats*.

"You, too." They both stared as Page wriggled away from her sister. Micki shook her head angrily. "Can you believe that?"

"Page looks pretty embarrassed," Bets answered.

"Not nearly as embarrassed as she should be," snapped Cindy. "Boy is that unfair."

Bets seemed unsure. "I guess."

Micki and Cindy were still watching Page as she staggered back to her seat. Jason was right there. He stretched out his arms and chanted,

"Log roll, log roll, Page Hain, log roll!" Kids shook their heads and batted him down, but when Page arrived at the end of his row, she was turned sideways and passed along like a department store mannequin. Everyone laughed, and a few dared Jason to roll Page down to the field. Instead, he lifted Page over his head, displaying her safe arrival, then engulfed her in his arms while the crowd boomed another rousing cheer.

"I can't take this," Micki said in a dead voice. "I've got to get out of here."

She headed toward the exit gate with Bets and the other girls following close behind.

Laurel had caught up with him.

In a cool corner where the grass was worn away and the top of the fence was torn, as if someone had fallen trying to climb over it. The halftime music was muffled out there. Cars cruised by, flashed their lights, and then moved on, leaving Jed and Laurel in the dark again.

The wind blew Laurel's hair and tousled her skirt. "What are you doing here?" she asked him. Until now, few words had seemed necessary besides "It's you" and "Hello."

Jed's bike leaned against the fence, and he was crouched next to it, tinkering with something in the motor. Laurel wondered how he could see. He'd insisted on staying there because he didn't want to be noticed. Because Page had been right, he wasn't supposed to be driving outside the Hain vineyard.

At first he didn't answer her, as if his bike was

much more important. Finally he tipped his face in her direction. His hair covered his eyes. "I saw you walking to the stadium."

"When?"

"Before."

"So?"

"I thought maybe, I don't know, we were . . . friends."

She wasn't sure if he was mocking her or not. "We are." She paused, making sure that her mind was working clearly. With Jed it was risky to be unthinking or offhand. "Why didn't you come up to me?"

"You disappeared." Jed went back to his bike. "You were with Page."

"Why don't I ever see you at school?" A car sped by, spooning light on them. Laurel still couldn't read Jed's expression.

"I told you before, I don't see people at school."

"Do you go?"

"Yes."

"To classes and everything?"

"Usually."

"Why don't I ever see you?"

"I don't hang out where I'm likely to be seen." He'd finally stopped tinkering. He rested his fists on his thighs and looked back at her. "Kind of like you."

Laurel's legs went wobbly. She made a semi-circle around him and leaned back against the fence, grateful that it was there to hold her up. "Where do you go, then?"

"Places. Off campus. During lunch, that is. After school I sometimes stay in the shop. I work on stuff."

"What kind of stuff?"

"Just stuff." He smirked. "Don't I seem like the kind of guy who stays after to work in the shop?"

It hurt Laurel to realize that he still needed to taunt and test her. "I don't know. I never took shop."

Her answer relaxed him. He flicked his hair off his forehead, almost smiled. "I guess you haven't. So what are you doing here?" Now it was a question contest. "Watching the game?"

"My dad wanted me to come. I wanted to keep Page company." She remembered the princess contest and wondered if Page was all right. She listened to make sure the halftime music was still playing. "You should get to know Page. She's not like her sisters."

"Could be."

"It's true. You could come with me. I'm meeting Page soon." She listened again. The brass and the drums were still droning on. "After the halftime."

Jed pointed to the stadium. "Over there?" He shook his head. "I'd rather stay out here. I'd always rather stay out here. Forever."

"I wouldn't."

Finally she had his full attention. She saw his India ink eyes as clearly as she saw the huge, dark sky.

"Why?" he said.

She had him. At last she'd offered a challenge,

and he was taking her up on it. Still, she hesitated. She hadn't even discussed this with Page, or with her father. She wasn't sure how to say it, or what good it would do.

"Why wouldn't you?" he repeated.

She turned away, felt rough metal fence against her arm and cheek. She was trembling, as if someone were peeling her skin off.

"What did you mean?"

"Nothing. Forget it."

"Tell me. I want to know."

"You don't."

"Tell me."

She spoke into the fence as if it were a microphone, or a mask. "Okay. Right after my mom left. Just last winter. I didn't cry. And I didn't talk to anyone for a while. Days. Weeks maybe, I don't remember exactly. Not hello. Not how are you. Nothing. It was this game I played — if I could not say a single word, somehow it would make things even."

"Even for what?"

"I don't know."

"What about school?"

"When teachers called on me, I shook my head. I carried this pad and wrote things down. Then I pretended I was sick, just stayed home and drew. My dad freaked out. Finally he started crying and said it wasn't fair, it wasn't fair for me to go away, too. And then, I don't know, I started talking again. That's when my dad decided we should move." She suddenly stopped, surprised that she'd said so much and not sure why she had. She wasn't shaking, though. Not anymore. Just scared. Scared that he wouldn't understand, or that he wouldn't care.

He stood up. He touched her shoulder to make her turn back to him. He looked at her. Really looked. It didn't matter that it was dark, because she knew that he was seeing much more than just her face. They didn't need light to find what they were looking for.

"I don't understand why the world is the way it is," Jed said. "School is this bizarre place that we have to go to every day, where all kids seem to care about is who has this and who lives there and wins this and loses that. It doesn't seem to have anything to do with what we feel inside."

The band music ended and was replaced by a low cheer.

Laurel remembered the stadium. Page and the contest and having to go back. She prayed for the band to start back up, for the halftime to last a few minutes longer. It was quiet. "I have to go. I promised Page."

He stood with his hands in his pockets, and she could feel his confusion as if it poured out of his whole body. She didn't know she'd have the nerve to do it until she was already close to him, and she'd slid her hands along the waistband of his jeans, so that their wrists touched . . . the back of hers to the inside of his. She laced her fingers through his empty belt loops and then she froze, scared again, embarrassed, not sure what to do next.

His head slowly fell until his cheek grazed her forehead and she felt his hair and his breath and the smooth warmth of his skin. He kissed her cheek, so lightly that she almost wasn't sure he'd done it. She lifted her face and then he kissed her mouth.

He kept kissing her until halftime was long over and she left him, racing back across the field.

CHAPTER 16

Simply getting out of the stadium that night wasn't enough for Micki. She found that she couldn't just leave. There was too much going on inside her and if she didn't take this feeling and do something with it, she just might go crazy.

Together the girls went toward campus. It was deserted, and they still heard the cheers from the football game as they roamed the halls, banging their fists against locker doors and giggling. But at the same time they were scared because they knew they were doing something not quite right. Micki kept having flashes of her mother rounding a corner to discover them. Ms. Susan Greene in her chic checked suit and little paisley tie, shaking her head and realizing that all those lessons — the French and the swimming and the violin — had been for nothing, because her daughter was on a Friday-night rampage with her friends.

"We're going to get in trouble," panted Alice. "I don't think we're supposed to be here."

"It's okay," argued her sister. "Don't be a wimp. The gates were open."

The girls stormed past the gym and the science labs, down the main hall, and over the quad. Bets had a little tear in her sleeve from where they'd stepped over the string and trampled through a rose bed. They kept moving.

"I'll never forget Page and Whitney down on that field as long as I live," Micki told the girls, getting more stirred up with each step. The feeling was so powerful that striding or stomping or pounding seemed the only way to let it out.

"Boy, would I like to pay her back," threatened Cindy.

They were just passing the sculpture garden, between a hall that led back to the math wing and one that led to the art rooms. Micki and Cindy hesitated, not sure which direction to head in next. "Which way?"

Bets stopped cold. Her cheeks were flushed and her hair flew into her face. "Maybe we should just go home," she said in a soft voice.

Cindy ignored her. "How about sneaking back to the Haunted House?"

"Yes!"

"That's a great idea."

"Mary Beth, it'll be scary."

"Wait a second!" Bets stamped her cowboy boot on the hard cement. When she had the other girls' attention, she took a deep breath to calm herself and tried to speak. "What — what are we doing? I don't like this. Let's go home . . . or somewhere."

Bets rarely got upset, and Micki didn't like seeing it. But going home was the last thing Micki wanted to do. Thinking about her parents and Peter was somehow mixed up with Page Hain and Jason Sandy, and it all combined to form that hot lump of pain inside her. She needed to keep moving.

"Oh, no!" warned Cindy. "Look who's coming. It's Mrs. Baughman."

"Get back. Quick!"

They plastered themselves against the wall of lockers while Mrs. Baughman, a math teacher, let herself into her classroom. As soon as her door closed and her light flickered on, they all burst out laughing, then clapped hands to their mouths. Micki's heart was slamming against her ribs.

A moment later Mrs. Baughman's door reopened and, forgetting to put out the light, the teacher calmly closed up and walked back toward the stadium. As soon as she was out of sight, Micki exploded in laughter again.

"Shhhh," ordered Cindy, giggling, too.

Micki couldn't stop. The giddiness was tumbling inside her, although it was neither joyful nor pleasant. That painful lump was turning to a breathless kind of excitement. As if she were a warrior. A spy. This feeling was very powerful. With this feeling she could do anything.

Suddenly Cindy brought her hands to her tanning-booth face and gasped. "Do you know where we are?"

Her astonished tone captured all of their attention.

"Where?"

Cindy was looking around now, making sure they were alone. "I don't believe it. This is so perfect."

"What!"

She curled a painted nail and drew them all in close. "See the last locker on the left? By Mr. Ritchie's art room. Number 409?" She led them over on tiptoes. "Guess whose locker that is?"

"Yours?"

Cindy shook her head. "Mine is there." She pointed to a blue enameled door in the middle of the bottom row. "But that one," she gestured back to 409, "belongs to none other than Page Hain."

"Are you sure?"

"I'm positive. I've seen her open it fifty times." Bets looked uneasy. "So?"

Cindy walked over to Page's locker. She put her ear to the door and spun the lock. "Anybody want to give cracking it a try?"

No one volunteered.

"Okay. I'll go for the first number." They held their breaths while Cindy slowly turned the dial. She closed her eyes and finally said, "There," responding to a click that no one else could hear. "You try," she told Micki.

Micki's hands shook. She'd heard about breaking into lockers, but didn't know that it could actually be done. She was terrified but strangely excited. She almost felt like she was outside herself, watching a movie of Michelle Madelyn Greene putting her ear to a cold metal door and twisting a knob. She felt a catch and heard a tiny, almost imperceptible *tick*. "I think that's it," she breathed.

Mary Beth rushed in for the last turn. She seemed the most experienced of any of them, and within a few seconds she was pushing up the metal slide and flinging open the door.

All five of them crowded around, very, very quiet. They examined the insides. For such an extraordinary-looking girl, Page had a pretty boring locker. There was a bag of potato chips inside, a pair of dirty gym shoes, an umbrella, and a stack of textbooks. The only picture taped to the door was a TWA ad with photos of European destinations. That was it.

They stood there, unsure of what to do next. Micki started to close the door.

"Maybe we should leave a message," Cindy decided. "Just a little reminder to let her know someone's been here." She fished a fat marking pen out of her shoulder bag. Leaning in, she scribbled WE WERE HERE in the corner of Page's locker.

The giggling started again, low and contagious. Alice went on lookout while Cindy handed Micki the marking pen.

"What should I write?"

Cindy threw her head back and grinned. "Anything you want."

HI THERE, PRINCESS, Micki wrote in letters slightly bigger than Cindy's. When she finished, she peeled away from the locker and started laughing again. Catching her giddiness, they all laughed harder.

Mary Beth grabbed the pen. "Come on, you guys," she said. "If we're going to do this, let's really do it." With a huge sweep, she drew X's up and down one wall. After more chuckling and guffawing, she went back and wrote PAGE HAIN SUCKS across the back.

Now it was Alice's turn. For once she didn't fight her sister. Laughing so hard that she was almost spitting, she added PAGE IS A PAIN IN THE HAIN.

Now they were howling. Cindy grabbed the pen back to add SUCK LIKE A DUCK, then Micki wrote TRAITOR, and Mary Beth penned KISS-UP and TWISTED SISTERS, and they all laughed even more.

Mary Beth handed the marking pen to Bets, and for a moment the laughter stopped. Bets looked from face to face to face with confused, watery eyes. Finally she gave the pen back to Mary Beth and walked away down the hall.

Page didn't like Redwood High at night. She still got lost in broad daylight and dreaded being asked to deliver a note to the office or drop a film back at the audiovisual office. A few weeks ago she'd had a stomache so bad she thought she'd scream, but who knew where the nurse's office was and who wanted to be an idiotic freshman and ask?

"Laurel," she called in a tiny whisper.

She kept walking. The one route she did know was to her locker, the central point of her high school life. She stomped across the quad and the dew soaked through her old deck shoes and made her feet freeze.

Halftime, she'd decided, had been the most humiliating fifteen minutes of her life. First, Jason pawing and breathing into her ear. Then posing on that ridiculous carpet like something in a K-mart window . . . and right next to Micki Greene, no less. Then Whitney grabbing her and starting that stupid cheer. And to top it all off, getting handed down a row of boys like an enormous leg of lamb. It was enough to make Page wish she hadn't been born a girl.

All Page wanted to do now was get back to her locker and find Laurel so they could call Laurel's father and go home. First thing Monday morning she'd drop out of that princess contest — no matter what Whitney said — and she'd figure out some way to make it through four years at this stupid school without ever getting near another contest . . . or football game . . . or gym class . . . or anything.

She passed the computer center, the art rooms. Finally she cut through the sculpture garden to get to her locker. As she did, she spotted Laurel rushing in from the other side. Laurel waved and hurried into the hall, the light from Mrs. Baughman's room spraying on her as she passed.

Laurel was really running as if she thought she were late, and yet her face had that dreamy, peaceful quality. Page couldn't help thinking that it was Laurel who was the beauty, not her. But Page couldn't focus very long on Laurel's face because she saw that there were other girls in the hall. Four of them standing in an awkward formation, as if Page had caught them in the middle of a secret.

Both girls heard muffled giggles, but something about this didn't feel at all light or carefree. Page recognized the Dubrosky twins, and figured that if the twins were there, Micki Greene was probably there, too. She blinked and saw that yes, Micki was there, and they were all standing around what Page realized was her own open locker.

From the other side of the hallway, Laurel's face hardened as she recognized the girls at almost the same time Page did. "What's going on?" Laurel called out first.

Another giggle, but other than that it was silent until there was a tiny plunk. Page and Laurel looked down to see a magic marker roll down the narrow hallway. Page felt the blood rush to her face and her fists tighten.

Cindy reached up to shut the locker door.

"Don't close it," Page ordered, as she walked forward. "You wanted me to see it, didn't you?"

No one answered.

Cindy moved aside and Page looked inside her locker. As she read the graffiti, she felt like someone was filling her body with lead. The four girls backed away as Laurel came up behind Page and put her hand on Page's shoulder.

Page's temper was turning red-hot. She felt as if she could explode and blow apart this entire stupid school.

Laurel squeezed her shoulder. "Just walk away, Page," she whispered. "Don't let them get to you. Just walk away."

Just at that moment there was another set of footsteps in the hallway. All seven of them froze as Mrs. Baughman appeared from the direction of the stadium. The teacher was jangling her keys and stopped when she saw the girls. Page half closed the locker door.

"Is everything all right, girls?" Mrs. Baughman asked in a pleasant voice.

Part of Page wanted to throw that locker door back open and show Mrs. Baughman just what Micki Greene — freshman class favorite — and her followers had done. But another part of her brain kept flashing the word "kiss-up" and thought about her sisters and the disgusting way they would have latched onto this opportunity. "Everything's fine," Page finally said. "We're just getting some books."

Mrs. Baughman smiled. "You should hurry back to the game." She slipped into her room and reappeared a moment later. "We're winning!" With that she locked up, headed in the direction of the parking lot, and disappeared.

Page pushed her locker closed and spun the lock. She was grateful now for Mrs. Baughman's interruption. It had given her a little time to cool down. Her fists were beginning to relax, and she didn't feel as if she was quite as likely to explode and blow everything around her to bits. Actually she felt almost numb. Heavy. As if she had cooled and turned into a statue.

Laurel pulled her away from the other girls. "Go on out to the parking lot," she told her.

"But why. . . ."

Laurel gently nudged her ahead. "Go on. I want to tell them something."

"You?"

"Please. It's important."

Page backed up into the hall. For some strange reason she suddenly knew that it was as important for Laurel to be the one to face them off, as it was important for her to fade into the darkness without a word. She stood in the shadows and waited.

Laurel took a deep breath.

When she finally turned back, the other girls were beginning to leave. They had their heads down, and they weren't saying anything. It was as though they were sneaking away. "Wait a minute," Laurel said.

All of them stopped.

Laurel slowly shook her head. "I hope you feel really good about this," she said in a low voice.

"Who asked you?" Cindy shot back.

Laurel ignored her and looked right at Micki. "I didn't know any of you in middle school. And you sure never made an effort to get to know me here. Maybe that's why I can see what you're doing. You're jealous. And the really stupid part is, you're jealous of all the wrong things. You don't deserve to be friends with Page."

"Who wants to be?" Cindy answered. "You're the ones who think you're so superior. Besides, we have each other."

For a moment there was silence. Laurel's lower

lip trembled but her eyes stared straight into Cindy's. "That's exactly what you deserve," was all she said. Then she turned and began walking. Eventually she disappeared into the shadows with Page.

For a few seconds the girls were quiet. Then Cindy folded her arms and began, "Well, lah-de-dah. . . ."

"Shut up, Cindy," Micki answered.

The girls looked at her for a moment, but not another word was spoken. Instead they began walking in the opposite direction down the hall.

CHAPTER 17

Micki barely slept that whole weekend. Every time she closed her eyes SUCK LIKE A DUCK would flash inside her head until she got this squeezed feeling, as if she'd been thrown in a trash compactor. She'd hug herself. She'd curl up. But the feeling hung on, and it was the opposite of being carried away and powerful. Now she felt deadened, dulled, scarcely able to move.

So before school on Monday, Micki forced herself to leave the house early. Earlier than she'd left since the very first day. Part of her decided that if she didn't leave at dawn she might never go anywhere again. Part of her just wanted out of the house before her parents started asking questions.

She jogged down the hill, letting gravity pull her faster and faster. The light was gray, the mist soft against her face. Micki passed house after sprawling-brick-and-redwood house, hardly looking at any of them until she came to the bottom.

"Now where?" she asked herself as she watched the traffic shoot past.

She was on Redwood Avenue, not far from school. But school was the last place she wanted to go. She'd talked to Doug and Carlos and Sarah and about a hundred other kids over the weekend. They discussed the float and the dance and what they were all going to wear for homecoming theme-dressing days. With each phone call Micki had felt more and more false. Because the twins hadn't called. Nor had Cindy. Nor had Bets.

Bets.

Micki was waiting for the light to change — thinking how she might wait there all day — when the Cotter Valley bus chugged into view. It was loud and gave off big clouds of exhaust, and all Micki could think was that it went past Bets's ranch on its way out of Redwood Hills. A second later she had dodged cars and grocery trucks and was dropping change in the fare box and staring out the bus window.

Soon busy downtown gave way to the open ranches and vineyards. Micki closed her eyes when they passed the Hain Winery, then tugged the cord about a half mile later and got off. The fog started to clear, and the sun began to show itself by the time Micki ambled up the long gravel driveway that led to Bets's plain split-level house. She hadn't even made it to the front door when Bets's dad, wearing overalls and riding what looked like a miniature tractor, intercepted her.

"Michelle," he called in a voice as happy and even-tempered as Bets's. He took out a handker-

chief and wiped his face with it. "What are you doing here so early?"

Micki looked past him at some equipment lying next to the driveway, and the scrubby land that looked so much rougher and messier than the pristine Hain vineyard. She could see two fat cows around the side of the house and hear several more nearby. "I thought Bets and I could go to school together."

Bets's father seemed a little puzzled. "She's been riding her bike most every day." He smiled. "But I'm sure you two can work it out. She's doing chores in the middle garage. Tell her it's almost time to get ready for school."

"I will."

Micki hurried around to the back of the house and found the metal-walled building where she could hear someone sweeping with a broom. She walked in as Bets was putting the broom away, her jeans soiled from the hard work and dust.

"Hi."

Bets looked up, surprised. "Hi."

There was a moment when they both were too embarrassed to look at each other. It didn't last very long and when they got over it, Bets boosted herself up on her dad's workbench. "How are you?" Bets said.

Micki looked around gloomily. Surely Bets knew how she felt, so she couldn't lie about it. But admitting it wasn't exactly easy. "Pretty awful, I guess."

Bets swung her legs slowly back and forth. Her cowboy boots occasionally kicked the paint cans and the pipe. "I know," Bets said. "I've been thinking about it all weekend."

"Me, too. It kind of makes me sick now."

Bets nodded. "How long did you stay after I left?"

"Not long."

"Did you write much more in her locker?"

"No." Micki went over and sat next to Bets. "I think we'd already done enough."

"Yeah."

They sat there for a moment in silence, both of them swinging their legs and tapping the cans and metal tubes in a sad, slow rhythm. "Why did you leave?" Micki asked finally.

Bets had such a hard time explaining things that it took her a long time to answer. She tossed her short blonde hair back and then shrugged. "I guess I've been thinking about doing stuff I don't feel right about. And realizing that, um, I don't have to. Sometimes I have to do things on my own. Does that make sense?"

"Sure." Micki hung her head and looked at the floor. "Are you mad at me?"

"I think, you know . . . I understand."

"Thanks."

Both girls stared across the shed for a few moments, until Micki finally slipped off the bench and walked around. She stuffed her hands in her pockets and kicked up puffs of sawdust. "I just want it to go away," she said, stamping the floor. "I wish I could just erase the whole thing! Make it like it never happened."

"But you can't."

Micki shook her hair. "When I think about

Page having to open that locker again today — "
Suddenly she stopped speaking. Her eyes opened
wide, and she stared at Bets's feet as if she'd just
seen a ghost.

"What?" Bets asked, hopping off the workbench and looking around. "What is it, Micki?"

Micki's mind was speeding. She was back on
track, and for the first time in days she felt like
smart Micki Greene again. She raced over to Bets
and pointed to the paint cans. "Do you think
your dad would mind if I took one of those cans
and a paintbrush? I'll replace it."

For a second Bets looked confused, then she
grabbed a half-full can of brick-red paint and
handed it to Micki. Both girls sorted through
some brushes on a shelf.

"Maybe. If I hurry."

"You could take my bike. The stuff will fit in
my basket."

"Thanks."

Micki took the paint can and both girls stared
at it.

Bets tugged on a strand of hair. "What if you
get caught?"

"Then I get caught."

"You might get in trouble."

"Then I get in trouble."

"Want some help?"

"No." Micki took a deep breath. "I think
maybe I need to do something on my own, too."

By lunchtime that same day, Page was carrying
four books: her notebook, her French book, her
English book, her history book. Carrying four

books all morning had made her shoulders ache and her backpack bulge, but the problem was much bigger than that. Page's real problem was that the four books she was lugging around were the wrong four books.

What Page needed were her algebra textbook and her language lab manual. She'd needed them over the weekend, and for the first time freshman year she'd had to tell her teachers that her homework hadn't been done. She'd considered saying my computer ate it, or my little brother puked on it — even though she had neither a computer nor a little brother. Anything seemed more believable than, Well, you see Mr. DeSalvio, my locker was desecrated by a bunch of girls who hate me, and I'm not quite up to opening it again.

Laurel had offered to fetch her books for her, but Page didn't want Laurel looking inside that locker, either. She was terrified that someone else might see or even that Laurel might believe some of those things if she read them again. Besides, as close as she was to Laurel, Page knew that this was her own problem.

So she'd left Laurel after gym class and headed over to the cafeteria. It was the first lunch period in weeks that she and Laurel hadn't eaten together, but Page sensed that Laurel understood, and that she might have been glad for the opportunity to sneak off and search for Jed. That was fine. Page couldn't think about Jed Walker right now. All she could think about was her locker and Micki and dropping out of the princess contest before someone did something even worse.

Page slowed down when she reached the entrance to the cafeteria, assaulted by the noise and the crowd and the salty tomato smell. She'd rarely been here since the first week, despite Whitney's objections that she was throwing away an important social opportunity. Snaking her way around tables and trash cans, Page was relieved to see that Whitney and the cheerleaders weren't at their usual center table. Good. Page hadn't mentioned dropping out of the contest to her sister. She knew Whitney would never allow it.

"Hi, Page," said Shelley Lara, a girl in her French class.

"Good luck with the voting tomorrow," said Shelley's friend.

"Thanks," Page mumbled, while noticing that Micki's crowd wasn't in the caf, either. Surely they were working on that float that everyone was so excited about. Even better, no Whitney and no *Micki Greene*. Now if she could just find Roger Sandler, head of the homecoming committee, and tell him that she was out of the contest, then this might be her lucky day.

Page veered away from the freshman tables when she spotted a group of junior boys. She figured they were juniors because they were sprawled across a tabletop, huddled around Jason Sandy, who was telling them something they all thought was very funny. Jason was dressed for the first homecoming theme day, Tacky Tourist Day. In his sunglasses, flowered shirt, and straw hat, he seemed even less trustworthy than usual. But Page figured that he could at least show her who

Roger was, so she shouldered her way through the crowd and over to his table.

"I know. It's outrageous," Jason was bragging. "I am Mr. Outrageous. What can I say?"

The boys applauded and laughed. Page waved to get Jason's attention, but the straw hat blocked his view of her and besides, he was much too involved with his buddies. Frustrated, she sat down at the adjoining table to wait.

"So she really went for it? What's her name?"

"Micki," laughed Jason, leaning forward and lowering his voice. "Michelle Greene. She's the most influential kid in the whole class."

Page held her breath. Her ears felt as if they were growing to the size of dinner plates. She quickly pulled out her French book and, burying her face in it, continued to listen.

"So I just dropped a few hints. . . ."

"Yeah, hints. Right, Sandy," another boy interrupted. "More like you whispered in her ear and got her motor running."

Jason howled. "Hey, look, guys, sometimes you have to play dirty." They all hooted. "But I'm telling you, it's gonna work. She changed the whole freshman float. She took my lawn chair idea, so now not only do we lose competition from the Class of '89, but they're practically giving it to us. It's like they're our intro . . . you know, the warm-up before you get to the real thing."

"All right, Sandy. We have this thing sewn up. So what are we going to do with that Haunted House?"

"Not so fast," Jason warned. "We still have to practice the brigade as much as we can. I expect to see you out on that back field after school every day."

"I don't know, Jason," joked a football player. "I think this whole farmhouse contest is a smoke screen. Admit it. You just go for freshman girls. I saw you with Hain's baby sister at the game."

"Give me a break, Warner. Hain's sister is a knockout. And besides, she's gonna win frosh princess and it can't hurt to have a girl like that on your side."

Now there was a chorus of macho hoots and suggestive laughs.

"Now, listen," Jason boasted, "if what I was really looking for was a girlfriend right now, I'd be hanging around those sophomore tables with Meg McCall. Woo. Now there's a girl worth. . . ."

Page didn't need to hear anymore. She stood up, kept her book in front of her face, and sidled her way back out to the main hall. The whole time her head was rocking. Micki Greene had been led on, used up, and she was about to be thrown away. Page wanted to take a gigantic magic marker and scribble that all over Micki's face.

Once Page hit the quad again, she wasn't sure where to go. She thought of going over to the float headquarters and facing Micki off, but there were only about ten minutes left of lunch. Besides, there was a homecoming powder puff football game out on the back field, which was right by industrial arts. Whitney was probably quarterback or something, and Page was still in no mood to see her sister. So she kept walking, past the art rooms, trying to decide what she should do and wishing that she could talk this over with Laurel. In the meantime she had to make it through three more classes.

"Darn," Page swore, remembering that she was supposed to have read the first five chapters of *Pride and Prejudice* for last-period English. Naturally the novel was in her locker. She peered down past Mrs. Baughman's room. Deserted. Maybe she could do it now, while everyone else was still at lunch. Run over, open her locker fast as lightning, grab the books she needed, and close it again without really seeing what was written inside.

"Here goes," she whispered.

She was out of breath when she reached number 409. Luckily there was still no one in sight. She spun the lock, but the door stuck. Page's heart sunk down to her toes. What had they done now? Filled her locker with garbage? Crazy glue? Cow manure? She gave one big tug and the door swung open.

Page stumbled back. Instead of dead animals or rotting food she was overwhelmed by the smell of fresh paint and the sight of four thickly covered brick-red walls. Only the floor of the locker, where there'd been no graffiti in the first place, was not painted over.

Sitting on that locker floor was a large paper sack. Still on guard, Page slowly unrolled the top and peeked in. Inside the sack were her books, her gym shoes, her umbrella, and a small bag of potato chips. She also found the TWA advertisement that had been taped to the inside of her door. It had been carefully removed and was rolled up atop the rest of her things.

"Laurel," Page said softly. "Thanks."

CHAPTER 18

"Yuck."

Micki looked at her fingertips and made a face. They were covered in soft, wet goo that was mushy like flour paste but stringy like taffy. Bits of shredded crepe paper and napkins clung to her hands like lint.

"Double yuck," Micki sighed.

She tried to flip the goo from her left hand, then redirected her attention to the chicken mesh that was stretched over pieces of plywood in the shape of a giant lawn chair. Micki was supposed to be glueing napkins and crepe paper in contrasting colors. At least that was the idea. She wanted it to look like a checkered pattern.

But it wasn't exactly working. In fact it wasn't nearly as contrasting as Micki's outfit. Doug had insisted that she get in the Tacky Tourist Day spirit. He'd loaned her his Hawaiian shirt after seventh period and then added a hula-girl tie after school. Between Doug's clothes, the dribbles of brick-red paint on her pink jeans, and the plugs of paste in her hair, she figured she looked like a creature out of a horror movie. She certainly felt like one.

Even though Micki had managed to repaint Page's locker without getting caught, she still felt uneasy. Part of it was that Page had sided against her classmates, and then gone on to steal Jason and probably the homecoming crown. Her sister had so blatantly advertised her as a candidate for princess that no one else had a chance. It seemed so unfair to Micki. That was why she still felt heavy and dull inside, all glommed up together like the goo on her fingertips.

"Forget about all this," Micki yelled at the ceiling. "Just work on the float."

Her words echoed off the ceiling of the shop building where the float was being constructed. Micki stared at the cable scattered on the floor, the motor that John Pryble had put together, the mess of float sketches, butcher paper, napkins, fabric, batteries, glue, wood, wire, and paint. She listened to her own voice come back, glad that she finally had a moment to yell out what she felt like yelling and not have to explain it.

Doug, Bets, and the others had just left on a food run to McDonald's. They'd wanted Micki to go, too, but she'd fended them off by arguing that the float might never get finished. The truth of the matter was that the float was in much better shape than she was. She was the one who still needed work.

Kneeling down again, Micki reached for another stack of blue napkins. She was slapping on more white glop when she heard the front door open and felt a draft.

She made her voice sound cheery and called out, "You guys back already?" The only response was the empty hum of the heater. "I thought you were going to stay there and eat. . . ." Her voice crumbled when she saw that it wasn't Bets at the door, or Doug, or any of her freshman friends. The only person in the room with Micki was Page Hain.

Page stepped in and shut the door. In her beige sweater and slacks she looked neither touristy nor tacky. She walked right over to where Micki was kneeling and peered down.

Micki went back to work on the lawn chair, as if it was the most important task in the world. "Hello," she said in a voice that didn't feel like hers.

Page stood spook still, her gray eyes fastened on Micki. "I wanted to see how the float was coming."

"Take a look. It's a free country."

Page slowly strolled around the float materials while Micki continued to paste. The freshmen had done a ton of work already. There was the lawn chair and a mechanical caveman, a long mural of Grizzlies in lawn chairs that would be stapled to the sides of Bets's father's flatbed, plus posters and banners made of felt. Micki couldn't help wondering if Page was impressed, if she was wishing she could have been a part of this, too.

"Very nice," Page commented.

"It's too bad you didn't come earlier. We don't need any more help now."

Page kept strolling. And she was getting this funny smile. "It looks like a lawn chair theme. I thought we were playing the Cotter Valley Cavemen."

"We decided to be creative."

"But I thought the theme was 'Cage the Cavemen.'"

"If you'd been to any of our meetings. . . ." Micki stopped. There was something in Page's steely eyes, in her smile and confident stance, that told Micki that Page had a very specific reason for being here, a reason that had nothing to do with her locker or the freshman float.

Page folded her arms and directed her eyes back to the float. "Maybe I should have gone to a few meetings," she said in a slightly bored voice, "but I heard all about it from Jason."

Micki's insides clamped down. So that was why Page was here. To get her revenge by throwing her romance with Jason in her face. Micki deliberately took a big hunk of goo and whacked it back onto the float. Page wasn't going to get to her . . . no way. Micki had done her penance already.

"Actually Jason didn't tell me directly," Page went on. "I overheard him telling a bunch of junior guys. He was saying how he led you on and got you to change the freshman float so the juniors could win that farmhouse contest."

Micki's hands stopped. "W-what," she stammered.

"That's why he paid attention to you, so he could get you to change the float." Page looked down, as if for a second she knew she might have gone too far. But then she looked right back at Micki. "He used you," she said.

"You're just saying this," Micki said. She threw a roll of crepe paper at the wall, but the end stuck to her palm and it unrolled across the floor. "You just know that Jason liked me, too."

Page's cheeks started to redden. "You think I like Jason Sandy? That creep?" Her coal-colored eyes were on fire, and Micki couldn't help remembering the way they'd gone at each other on the soccer field. "You think I liked having him paw me just because he thought I might win homecoming princess? Because that's the only reason he paid any attention to me, either."

Micki was on her feet. "What about princess? What about having your sister pull strings for you and not doing anything for your class? What makes you think you can get away with that?"

"You know something? Do you know something?" Page shouted. "I agree with you. I don't deserve to be elected anything. And I was going to drop out of that contest because I don't want anything to do with this stupid class. But I didn't drop out. You know why?"

"Why?"

"Because then you might win. And I don't want you to win anything. Not after what you and your friends did to my locker!"

Both girls were silent. Micki could feel her throat tightening, and she wiped her forehead with the back of her arm. She'd always thought she was the most together person in her class, and now she was realizing that she was the biggest fool of all. Finally she looked back at Page. "I'm sorry about your locker," she mumbled. "We got carried away."

"Oh, you did?" Page picked up a stack of napkins and pitched them into the air. They floated down like giant butterflies. "Well, I can get carried away, too." Suddenly there was a crack in Page's fury and her eyes widened. "Have you been back to my locker since Friday night?" she asked quickly.

Micki didn't answer.

Page waited for a moment, staring at Micki. When Micki still wouldn't respond, Page's anger returned. "So what are you going to do now? What are you going to do about your float and all your loyal friends?"

"I'm going to . . . I'm. . . ."

"What? Tell me. What are you going to do?"

"I don't know."

"You don't, do you!"

"No . . . I. . . ." Sobs erupted. Micki looked around at the banners and the signs and the papier mâché, all decorated with Jason's idiotic lawn chairs. Two months of planning and begging for materials, two weeks of working before and after school. Useless. Worse than useless. But what was she going to do now? Homecoming was Friday and her whole class was depending on her. She was the one who got them all hopped up about the farmhouse contest in the first place.

Micki picked up the lawn chair that she'd been building so carefully and slammed it down on the concrete. There was a sharp *clack* as an arm broke in two. Napkins and crepe paper fell off. John Pryble's motor thunked to the floor. "I HATE HIM!" Micki cried. "I hate Jason so much. Why did he do this to me?" She kicked the lawn chair again and the base splintered down the middle.

Suddenly Micki realized that Page was right next to her. There were tears streaming down her face, too. Her features were so distorted and angry that she barely looked pretty anymore.

"You hate Jason?" Page cried. "Well, I hate Jason more. And I hate Whitney and all her stupid friends. I hate Julianne. I hate them telling me what to do and I hate being just like them."

"It's not fair!" Micki screamed.

"I hate them!" Page echoed. "IT'S NOT FAIR!!"

Suddenly they were both kicking what was left of the lawn chair. Another plank of wood clunked off and then a slice of chicken wire unraveled. They went wild, tearing and wrecking and breaking until the lawn chair was just a mass of dusty paper and splintered wood and bits of wire and paste. There was almost nothing left of it, and Micki and Page both fell onto their knees, sifting through the wreckage. They were looking for one more intact piece to rip to shreds. They were no longer crying, but heaving deep shaky breaths and wiping off their faces with dirty hands.

Just then the front door to the shop opened. Doug, Bets, Sarah, Paul, and all the rest of them barreled in. "Hey, Mick," Doug was yapping, "I know you said you didn't want anything, but I brought you a burger and fries because I figured you were really telling me a huge lie and. . . ."

Doug froze, mystified. He and the rest of the freshmen came to a screeching halt, plowing into one another as they stopped to stare.

"WHAT'S GOING ON?"

Micki looked at Page. Page looked back at her. They were both sitting in the rubble, looking as if they'd just been through a tornado. Page's hair was full of paste now, too, and there was a scrap of felt sticking to her forehead. She picked up a broken piece of wood, and then let it drop back onto the concrete floor. She looked at Micki again, and then she started to laugh. A deep, broad, chesty laugh.

Micki stared. She felt like yelling, *How dare you?* But then a strange thing happened. Micki didn't know why, but she began to giggle, too. While the rest of the freshmen stared at the two of them as if they'd gone totally and completely nuts, she and Page laughed harder and harder. Laughing so hard, in fact, that they began crying some more. Then they ended up by laughing again. The whole thing suddenly seemed very, very funny.

An hour later, reality set in. About ten of them had stayed and they sat in a circle around Micki, staring at the remains of two months of useless work. Micki had explained everything. What had been funny wasn't so funny anymore. The laughing had stopped.

Page sat across from her. Micki wasn't sure

why Page was still there, but she was. Cindy had gone home long ago, but the twins were sticking it out, as were Paul and John, Carlos and Sarah. And of course, Doug and Bets.

They all stared at the mess, which now included the wrapping from Micki's hamburger, and pieces of torn paper that people would occasionally pick up and bat around like balloons.

"I guess I should go," Page said after a while, breaking a long silence. She slowly got up and reached down to brush off her trousers. "I'm supposed to go over to my friend Laurel's house." Everybody watched her. No one said anything. "Do you want me to help clean up?"

Micki shook her head.

Page shrugged. "If you want me to help rebuild your float, I guess I should."

Micki looked at her and then looked back at the floor. "You don't have to do that," she said flatly.

"Well, maybe we should just forget about the parade after all this. It's probably better that way."

"Maybe."

There was silence again. Page lingered. People moved uncomfortably. Bets slid her arm around her ankles and lowered her head. Things felt bad.

Finally Doug slapped his fist into his hand. He'd been uncharacteristically quiet through this whole thing, and Micki wanted to keep it that way. The last thing she needed right now was to hear Doug's jokes. But this time he didn't make a funny face or even crack a smile. He got up slowly. "We let them beat us," he said in a low voice. "If we don't show up at the parade, it's the same as if we went ahead with Jason's float."

Micki rolled her eyes. "Doug, how can we enter the parade? Look around you."

"Who cares about this float? It wasn't really our float anyway. Why don't we just start over and make another one, a float that really represents us?"

Page took a step back into the shop.

"How are we going to do that?" Micki argued. "We have three days. How are we going to get new materials and make a completely new float by Friday?"

"I don't know," Doug said, starting to pace back and forth. "But I know we can do it. We were always good at making the best of things at Portola."

A few others smiled and nodded.

"Why can't we do it?" Doug said, getting more excited.

"Yeah," cheered John.

"Why don't we make a new one?" said Alice and Mary Beth at the same time.

Paul sat up, too. "I can find new supplies."

"That lawn chair idea was dumb anyway."

"Yeah. We can go back to our old idea."

"Or make up a better one."

Micki looked at her friends and almost started crying again. But she didn't feel despair this time, she felt affection. The Class of '89 that could turn the most boring assembly into a wild party and a wild party into a Mardi Gras. It was the same class that the older kids had been trying to run down ever since they'd started at Redwood. She knew Doug and Paul and the rest of them were right. The worst thing they could do was give up now. But for some strange reason, the final person Micki looked to for approval was Page.

Page looked right back at her and said, "There's a ton of extra paint and wire and all kinds of stuff at our vineyard."

"Well," Micki said, with a big grin. "What are we waiting for?"

Everybody went crazy.

CHAPTER 19

"WATCH THE JUNIORS MAKE THE GRADE.
Watch the juniors make the grade.
REDWOOD HIGH LAWN-CHAIR BRIGADE.
Redwood High lawn-chair brigade.
RIGHT FACE.
LEFT FACE.
PARAAAADE REST!"

Laurel and Page sat on the edge of the back field, watching Jason and the juniors rehearse the infamous lawn-chair brigade. It was the day before homecoming, and Jason screamed like a drill sergeant with a crew of raw recruits. Both girls cringed as Jason belted out orders, forcing his troops to regroup and begin again.

"Boy, will I be glad when this week is finally over," Laurel sighed.

Page nodded. "I know what you mean. I never thought I'd say it, but after this, I think I'll appreciate boring, normal school."

"Me, too."

"Still, I have to admit, even I'm starting to get into it."

Laurel picked blades of grass and scattered them. For a moment she didn't say anything. "I told you winning princess wouldn't be so awful."

"When they announced my name yesterday, I kind of felt sick to my stomach. It's more than that, it's . . . oh, no!" Page clapped her hands over her ears. "Here he goes again!"

Laurel frowned. "Oh, no."

"COME ON, YOU JOKERS!" Jason screamed. "At least learn your right from your left. Watch me."

Page and Laurel watched as Jason demonstrated a proper parade rest — quickly opening and setting down the lawn chair, trotting around it, sitting, and pretending to be taking a snooze. Jason ordered his troops to try again, and when they didn't do it right, he yelled some more.

"I don't think something can be funny when you have to work that hard at it," Laurel observed. "Do you?"

"Probably not. I do like his lawn chair, though."

"Yeah."

Page giggled. Jason had his famous lawn chair, which was red-and-blue checked with the Grizzly paw print on the back and on the seat.

"So how's the float going?" Laurel asked,

glancing over at the two industrial arts buildings. The late afternoon sun cast a long shadow over the metal grooves.

"Pretty well, I think." Page was on a break from float detail. She'd been working along with her class all week. She'd barely seen Laurel, except to ask her to contribute a few sketches, which Laurel had generously done. Page hadn't asked Laurel to come over to the float headquarters because she doubted that Laurel would go . . . and because Page still couldn't quite believe she went over there herself.

"Do you think the new idea will work?"

"Shhhh!" Page warned, looking around furiously. "The upperclassmen can't know. No one who isn't a freshman can know we changed it. Especially creepy Jason. It has to be a surprise."

"Don't worry. I don't have a lot of upperclass friends to tell."

Page nudged her and smiled. "I know."

Laurel stared down at her lace-up boots. "So they really like my drawings?"

"Of course! But they don't know that some of the cartoons are supposed to be them." Laurel had produced poster-sized sketches of bears with humanlike heads. Only Page recognized that Micki was represented in those cartoons, along with Betsy Frank and herself.

"They didn't figure it out?"

"No." Page found an apple in her backpack and handed it to Laurel. "But you know something? Some of those people are so crazy, I don't think they'd care."

Laurel shook her head and handed the apple back. "I still can't believe you go there every day after what they did to you."

"I sort of can't believe it, either."

"Do you really like them?"

Page thought for a minute. "I don't not like them. Not anymore. I'm not really sure. The one thing I do feel is that with this whole princess thing, at least I should do something to deserve it. Does that make any sense?"

"I guess." Laurel looked off at the shop buildings again. The breeze tossed her hair and she let a few strands fall over her face. She seemed a little limp today. Sad. "So what are they doing — I mean, with the posters I made?"

Page bit into her apple with big, hungry bites. "Now they just have them tacked up in the shop. I think they plan to staple them to the sides of the flatbed. See, we're making all the costumes and posters and props and stuff now, but we won't be able to put it together until tomorrow. It'll be right before the parade, when we have the truck and the flatbed trailer." Laurel nodded, but Page wasn't sure she was really listening. "Laurel, are you okay?" she asked quietly. She put the apple away and touched Laurel's wrist.

"What? Oh, sure."

"Honest?"

Laurel tried to smile. "Honest."

Page wondered what was going on with Laurel, as Jason bossed his brigade again. She knew that sometimes Laurel just got sad, probably because of her mother. But part of the reason that Page couldn't quite read her was that she hadn't seen

Laurel all that much since Monday. And Laurel didn't have any other friends at Redwood to talk to — except the invisible-man Jed, whom she hardly ever saw. Then it dawned on her, and Page suddenly felt incredibly slow and stupid. How could she not see that the one real friend she'd made in this crazy mess called high school felt left out?

Page stood up and held out her hand. "I have to go back and work on the float. You come, too." She pulled Laurel up.

Laurel's green eyes seemed to get even greener behind her glasses. "Me? I don't want to go over there with all those kids. Not after what they did."

"Look, who did they do it to? Me, right?"

"Yes."

"And who told them off? You, right?"

"Yes."

"And so how can you let me go back there by myself, when I obviously need you to protect me."

"Oh, sure."

"Would I lie to you? Have I ever lied to you?" Laurel was smiling.

"Are you my best friend, or aren't you?"

Laurel stopped cold and looked at Page with her intense, serious eyes. "Am I?"

"Of course you are," Page said. After a moment she started tugging her again. "And a best friend would never desert me at a time like this. Would she?"

"Okay." Laurel laughed. "Okay."

Jed just wanted his motorbike to be fixed. He'd endure anything for that. Not having the auto shop to himself. Other kids roaming in and out, using tools and making corny jokes. That upperclass yell leader Jason, out on the back field, hollering at his classmates and forcing them to fold patio chairs. Jed had even put up with Jason shouting at him when he'd dared to cross the lawn during one of Jason's practices. Then later Jason had been in the parking lot with his football pal Gus Baldwin, and they'd both sneered when Jed walked by. But now Jed was getting close. A few more cranks with his wrench. . . .

"Nada." Jed swore. The part had broken. He put the wrench down and turned the light on over the shop counter. His work wasn't done yet.

He thought about what it would be like when this clutch was right and he was on that bike again. Even if he got caught riding illegally on the street, his uncle wouldn't care. His uncle never cared much what he did. Besides, he could always ride it at the vineyard. There, nobody could catch him.

"Yo," someone yelled in a dopey voice. Jed kept his eyes on his work while a lanky kid from his gym class loped in. He had short hair with a skinny blond ponytail, and right away he started drumming the counter, singing to himself.

"Do you need something?" Jed finally had to ask.

"Yo. I do. Hey, I know you from PE. Doug Markannan." Doug put his hand out to shake. Whe Jed didn't shake it, Doug shrugged and drummed the counter again. He watched Jed work. Jed couldn't help a slight smile. Doug always wore the craziest clothes for gym and drove the teacher nuts.

"Do you really know what you're doing?" Doug asked.

Jed grabbed a rag and left his work to clean the oil off his palms. He could put up with people going in and out and upperclass Jason yelling and Gus putting him down. But somebody staring at him from two inches away was more than even Jed could ignore. "Yes, I do."

Doug backed off. "Hey, that's cool. I don't mean to bug you or anything. It's just that I invented this thing for our freshman float, you know, next door. It's this sort of bear paw thing that could move. It's attached to a pulley, but we built a motor to make it work and now the alternator won't work."

Jed stopped listening because Doug had left the door propped open, and Jed had just caught a flicker of pale hair and a lacy old-fashioned skirt. Laurel. She was with Page. Whenever he saw Laurel with Page, he made a quick exit in the opposite direction. But this time there was nowhere to go.

"So, do you think you might be able to come over and take a look at it?" Doug was still blathering.

"Hi," said Laurel.

Jed started putting his tools away. Actually, he didn't put them away, but rearranged them and pushed them around on the counter. Anything to avoid looking at the two girls.

Laurel came closer. As much as he needed to

avoid her he couldn't keep his gaze away for long. He hadn't kissed very many girls in his life. He hadn't realized how strongly it would make him feel. He turned and they looked at one another for what must have seemed to the others like a very long time.

Page came over, too. Jed took a rag from his pocket and began wrapping up the clutch from his bike.

"Hi," Page said, sounding almost as tentative as Laurel had.

Jed felt everything freeze up inside. In spite of what Laurel had told him, he couldn't believe that Page was any different from her sisters. When they ran into him at the vineyard, they acted like he was as important as another tied-up vine.

"I'm Page," she told him, as if he didn't know. "It's weird that we live so close to each other and we've never talked." She looked back at Laurel as if to say, Am I doing this right?

"Weird," Jed repeated. "That's one way of putting it." He noticed that Doug was still standing there, watching quietly and with interest.

Page gave a funny, self-conscious laugh. "I guess I just wanted to say hello. That's all. Since we go to the same school now."

Jed looked into her gray eyes and for a split second allowed himself to see the warmth and the intelligence and a little bit of fear. Then he broke away and spoke to Doug. "Why don't you take me over and show me that pulley thing. Maybe I can fix it."

Doug led the way, and Jed didn't look back. He made himself not think about Laurel, and when the boys got to the freshman float room, things were crazy enough so that there wasn't time to think about anything. There were more than forty kids packed in there, all fiddling with wire and lumps of cardboard, banners and papier mâché, and scraps of dark brown fake fur. From what he could tell, nobody was bothering to sneer or make comments or really notice him at all, other than to acknowledge that he was just another freshman. They were all too busy.

"Here," Doug called, waving him over.

Jed saw a simple motor in a shoe box, like the ones he had built as a little kid. It was running a contraption that rigged a papier mâché bear paw to move up and down. Right away Jed saw the problem. It took only a minute to fix.

"Okay," Jed said. "I'm done. Let 'er rip." When Doug pulled on the cord again, the bear paw made a graceful sweep.

"Whoa," Doug cried happily. "Thanks."

"Sure."

That was when Jed realized that he had an audience. Probably eight or nine kids were standing around. He recognized a punk-looking girl from his English class who sometimes wore a Walkman, and a blond guy who was with him in fourth period shop. But most important, Laurel and Page were standing there, too.

"You fixed it?" Laurel asked with a smile.

Jed shrugged. "I guess. We both fixed it," he said, referring to Doug.

Doug laughed. "I didn't fix it. He did."

"Well, it's great," Page answered.

Jed came down from the float, leaving the congratulations for Doug. But when he reached the door, Doug called out to him. "So will you meet us tomorrow, on the street by the main entrance? I know when we put that pulley on the float the same thing'll happen. Just meet us after the spirit assembly. We'll be out of class anyway."

Jed stood in the doorway wondering why he hadn't taken one more step before Doug had been able to call him back.

Doug was waiting for an answer. They were all staring at him, waiting for an answer. Page was waiting. So was Laurel.

"Okay," Jed mumbled. "All right. I'll meet you."

"All right!" Doug cheered.

Jed hurried out and broke into a run, racing blindly onto the back field, just because he had that much energy to use up. That much tight, fizzy, good energy. He ran the way he rode his bike in the vineyard — just for the feel of it. He couldn't believe that he'd agreed to meet them tomorrow. He couldn't believe that he'd gone over and joined his class. He couldn't believe that he felt this happy. This free. It just seemed that whenever Laurel Griffith was near him, anything was possible.

CHAPTER 20

"Freshmen, meet the freshmen. We're the modern Stone Age family...."

It was the Friday of the parade, and Doug was dancing on the top of Bets's father's flatbed, grinding his feet and singing to the tune of the Flintstones.

"Are those the words?" Sarah Parker asked. She wasn't wearing her Walkman as she walked around making a last-minute check of the freshman float.

"I don't know," giggled Mary Beth.

"Me either," agreed Paul.

"Somebody run to audiovisual and turn on the TV and look for a rerun," Doug suggested.

"Dougie, knock it off."

WHONNNK!

Micki looked up at their float and glared but she couldn't hold it for long. She immediately burst out laughing. Doug looked just so . . . so . . . well, caveman. There was no other word to describe him. There was something definitely prehistoric about him. He fit in perfectly with the theme of the revised freshman float — SEND THE CAVEMEN BACK TO THE STONE AGE. His long legs and arms were almost totally exposed in his furry suit. It was pretty nippy, but Doug wasn't worrying about it, or even acting like this was any different from anything else he ever wore around school. It was a good thing, because Micki was positioning and repositioning him with all the other characters on the float. They'd worked out a tableau, and Micki wanted them all in place before they started down Redwood Avenue for the parade.

"Okay," she said into the megaphone, which amplified her already-vibrant voice, "now I need the rest of the cavewomen."

Instantly the twins, Sarah, and Bets assumed their poses. In the middle was Carlos in the Redwood mascot's Grizzly costume.

"Good. Pebbles? Where's Pebbles?"

"Here."

Page came forward and was truly a sight to behold. The freshman princess was done up in a costume that was almost an exact replica of Doug's except that she also had a silly ribbon around her head that tied on a giant papier mâché bone. But besides making everyone laugh, Page's outfit also made everyone's jaw drop — Page was gorgeous.

"Okay, Page and Doug," Micki said into her

megaphone. "Page, you're pulling Doug by the hair, dragging him back to your cave."

Doug objected. "Can't we do it the other way around?"

"NO!" shouted about five girls at the same time.

"Just thought I'd ask."

"Ready," Page said, tugging Doug's rat tail and giggling.

"Is this going to work?" Micki called out to anyone who might be listening.

The person who answered her was Laurel Griffith. "I think so," Laurel said in a soft voice. She was standing just to Micki's left, checking her drawings, which were tacked to the sides of the flatbed.

"Your posters are great," Micki told her.

"Oh. Thanks."

But when Micki looked back at the float, she saw that Doug and Page had broken their poses. He was fiddling with the mechanical bear paw, while Page stood next to him, watching with a worried look.

"Has anybody seen the guy who knows how to work this?" Doug yelled into the freshman crowd.

"Jed," Laurel and Page corrected.

"Oh, yeah. Jed Walker," Doug remembered. Somebody at the end of the street had just tooted a whistle, and Bets's father was leaning out of the pickup, asking when they would be ready to take off. Doug was starting to shiver now, too. "I wish he'd show up."

A junior carrying a lawn chair crashed into Laurel, and she moved aside to avoid a senior

215

whose face was painted with red-and-blue glitter. "I'll see if I can find him."

Laurel made her way through the crowd, even though she wasn't sure exactly which way to go. It seemed like the entire high school was out here on the street, plus parents and teachers, townspeople getting seats for the parade, and even a couple of police cars. "JED!!" Laurel yelled into the cold clear sky.

Then Laurel felt a warmth at her back and even though he didn't say anything, she knew he was there. She turned around and his dark blue eyes took her in from her ankles to the top of her head.

Jed was out of breath. He wore only a white T-shirt and jeans, but his face was damp with sweat and he was flushed. "Here," he said, handing her something that at first she couldn't recognize. It was red and blue and square and had a paw print emblem on it. "I grabbed it on the way over here. I thought maybe one of you could use it." He wiped his forehead, then spotted Doug calling him over from atop the float, and jumped up to help him.

"What's that?" Micki said, staring at what Jed had given her.

Both girls realized what it was at the same time. Laurel pulled it open, and she and Micki stared. It was Jason Sandy's lawn chair. His beloved, spirit-color-coordinated, Grizzly-paw lawn chair. Just as quickly, Laurel snapped it shut again and hid it behind her.

"We're getting this under control!" Doug called down.

"Good," Micki yelled back, beginning to feel a wonderful kind of excitement. This was a little like that dangerous thrill she'd felt the night they'd trashed Page's locker — only much more pleasant . . . and sane. She looked around at Laurel and the crowd. The whole scene was pretty nutty, but also uniquely Class of '89. They'd done it. All of them. Together. They'd really done it.

"What should we do with the chair?" Laurel whispered.

"I don't know." Micki glanced up at Jed, who'd finished fixing the bear paw and was jumping back off the wagon. He stepped back and the crowd swallowed him up. "I just hope no one saw Jed take it."

But there was no more time to worry about Jed and the lawn chair. A group of teachers and parents were strolling along with clipboards, observing each float and judging it before the parade began. And Micki tensed as she realized that Jason was heading her way, chatting with the judges and trying to charm them.

"You have to judge ours as we're moving. That's the whole point of the lawn-chair brigade," Micki heard him say. She cringed at the peppy sound of his voice. He had on his lawn-chair brigade T-shirt and Tom Cruise sunglasses. When he spotted Micki, he waved and cut over to join her.

"Hey, Micki," Jason said. He winked and tousled her hair, but at the same time he glanced around as if he was looking for something.

Micki'd seen him a few times since Monday, and although it made her ache to look at his face

217

now, she'd gotten some satisfaction out of leading him on all week by telling him that his float idea was working out just fine.

Jason was bobbing up and down now, looking around so frantically that he didn't seem to notice the freshman float at all. Micki waited.

"Have you seen Gus Baldwin?" he asked her. "You know Gus, captain of the football team?"

"I don't think so."

"Crap." Jason pasted on a yell leader smile and waved to another of the judges. "Somebody lifted my lawn chair," he told Micki in an urgent voice.

Micki gasped. "Really?"

"Gus saw who did it. I sent him to get it back for me." Jason checked his watch. "I wish he'd hurry up."

Micki couldn't wait any longer. "So how do you think our float turned out?" she asked him.

Jason barely looked at first, he was obviously so confident that Micki had followed his orders. When he finally did take in the new freshman float, his jaw went slack. All the charm and vivacity drained out of his puppy eyes until they looked to Micki like two brown rocks. Even his adorable curls seemed to droop over his ears. "What happened to the lawn-chair float?"

"Lawn chairs?" Micki repeated, full of mock innocence. "Gee, I don't know. We figured this school had too many lawn chairs already."

Now Jason's rock-hard eyes were turning muddy and mean. But before Jason could come back at her, Whitney flew over. She was in her cheerleading outfit and had a bright red paw print drawn on her cheek. "Jason, would you get your brigade moving?" she snapped. "We're supposed to start moving on the sophomore float, but we can't go until you stupid juniors move ahead of us."

Jason was still staring at the freshman float, as if by staring at it he could transform it back to what he'd hoped it would be. Whitney glanced over it briefly, then turned back to prod Jason again. But her gray eyes did a strange double take and her fluffy hair whipped around until she stood staring up at the freshman float, too.

"Hi, Whitney," Page called down in a goofy voice. She was holding Doug by the hair, while the mechanical bear paw moved gracefully up and down. She giggled; a lovely, free giggle.

"Oh, my God, Page," Whitney heaved.

Mary Beth waved to Whitney, too. "Sorry you didn't make sophomore princess," she said, "but I think Joanne Fantozzi was a good choice. Don't you?"

Whitney's face began to turn scarlet. She glared up at Page and brandished a creamy fist. "Page, get down from there. You look ridiculous."

Page shrugged while Doug started singing the Flintstones' song again. "I think I'm just fine."

Whitney looked like she was about to take off and break the sound barrier. She came right up to the edge of the wagon. "Get down from there, Page," she threatened. "If you are seen like that, there is not a single person in my class who will ever talk to you again."

Page started to sing along with Doug. "Freshmen, we're the freshmen. . . ."

"Page!"

WHONNK!

Whitney almost fell over in shock at the blast from Doug's saxophone. A shrill whistle sounded out on the street.

"That's it!" Micki shouted. "Everybody away from the float who's not a caveperson. Let's go!"

The flatbed jolted and began to move.

"You'd better get back to your own float," Page yelled down to her sister. " 'BYE!"

All the freshmen on the float were singing and waving until, at last, Whitney gave up and stormed back to her classmates. At the same time Jason was fidgeting like a madman, still looking for Gus, while he heard his lawn-chair brigade taking off without him.

"Nuts!" Jason yelled out.

"You'd better get going," Micki told him. "They're leaving without you."

"You'll let me know if you see Gus or my chair?"

Micki smiled sweetly. "Absolutely."

Jason took off, and a moment later Micki and Laurel took off, too. They ran ahead, Jason's chair tucked under Laurel's arm, ducking through the crowd until they made it out onto the street. When they were finally on the first block of the parade route, they jogged past the barriers the police had put up to block off traffic. They sat together on the curb.

They were just in time. The senior float had just passed, followed by the Pep Club and the football team. Next came the lawn-chair brigade. Jason led them with a furious scowl, presenting his maneuvers with a very unmacho pink patio chair.

"HEY, JASON, GREAT FLOAT!" Micki screamed. She took his chair from Laurel and held it up high. "WAS THIS WHAT YOU WERE LOOKING FOR?"

Jason shot up in the middle of a parade rest. He whipped off his sunglasses and his mouth opened in rage. But just then the judges walked by him with their clipboards, and he had to smile again and put his troops through their paces.

"Hmm," Laurel said to Micki. "You'd think he was upset or something."

"Or something," Micki giggled.

She flung the chair down and both girls squeezed into it, sitting on the sidewalk with the other freshmen to watch the rest of the parade.

An hour later the blaring and the honking and the hooting had faded away. Traffic was flowing down Redwood Avenue again, and the last scraps of crepe paper and wire were being picked up. Micki and Bets, Page and Laurel ambled across the quad, sometimes skipping, and hummed the tune from the Flintstones, reveling in their class's success.

"I still can't believe we won," Micki giggled.

"I think we were the first freshman class to win anything at a Redwood homecoming," said Bets.

"Well, it is only the second year of the school," Page pointed out.

"Still," Micki grinned.

They laughed and kept walking, entering the main hall and heading past the attendance office.

Laurel was right with them, amazed at how at home she felt. They'd all agreed that they weren't sure about attending the homecoming game, and were even more iffy about the dance. So they'd decided to meet at Laurel's apartment before the game, just to check in and to decide whether or not to go.

Laurel was thinking about her dad and how excited he would be that she actually had three friends. She was also thinking about how strange it was that she'd been able to forgive Micki and Bets. Maybe that was what it was all about for her . . . learning to forgive. To forgive her mom for leaving. To forgive herself for not wanting to leave with her.

That was when she spotted Jed again. He was inside a small room next to the attendance office. Jed was alone. He sat in there with his hair half covering his face. As soon as she saw him, she hung back and told the others to go on without her.

"I'm going to stick around for a few minutes and get some things done," she told them. "I'll see you later at my apartment."

"Okay."

"We'll come over after dinner."

They were too giddy to question her. They waved, assured her they would see her later, and kept going.

Laurel waited until they were gone, then went into the small office. Jed was sitting in one of those yellow maple chairs, but not with his legs sprawled out as usual. He was curled up, so that the heels of his tennis shoes were just touching the edge of the chair. His head was down, too, so he didn't see her. There was a muddy rip in the shoulder of his T-shirt.

For a second Laurel was so happy to see him again that she didn't even think about it. But then she realized that something was very wrong.

"It's me," she said.

Jed raised his head from his folded arms, blinked once in the light, and then stared at her. He didn't say a word and eventually he put his head back down.

"Do you have a class in here?" she asked.

"I don't belong to any class."

They were back to ground zero. She reached out to touch Jed's hand, but he flinched and moved away. Laurel took a big breath, holding back the hurt. "Are you in trouble?"

"You could say that."

Laurel looked down and bit her lip. For some reason, all the happiness of the last couple of hours was draining out of her and was being replaced by a feeling that was echoey and hollow. "Why are you in here?"

"Detention," he finally answered, still not looking at her but trying to sound like he was proud of it.

"Where's the teacher?"

"Went to clean up the parade. But he'll be back. He promised me he would."

"What happened?"

Jed pretended he didn't hear.

"Was it because of that lawn chair?"

"You could say that."

Laurel looked at his shoulder again. There was

a scratch under the tear and a tiny line of red. "Did you get in a fight?"

"You could say that."

She closed her eyes and sat back on a desktop. She couldn't believe that after everything that had happened, she and Jed were back to square one. "With Jason Sandy?"

Finally Jed looked up. He scoffed. "He sent his henchman, Mr. Football."

"Where's he, then? Didn't he get detention, too?"

"You don't get detention when you're captain of the football team. Not on homecoming." Jed stared for a second at the wall behind Laurel and then looked at her. He took one foot off the edge of the chair and stretched out. "The whole thing was stupid. I should never have gotten involved in the first place. I should have stayed out there forever, just like I said."

Laurel couldn't believe that the old Jed had come back, and that trying to get through to him was like chiseling with a hammer. "Don't do this, Jed," she urged. "Go tell them off. Or forget it. Let it pass."

"Leave me alone," was all he would say.

But Laurel understood much more. Jed wanted to stay there on the outside. He'd taken a step in, but when things looked tough again he was just backing up. No forgiveness. No compromise. His toughness was as fake as fool's gold.

He would no longer look at her. Laurel felt a tear threaten and she knew that if she stayed with him she would have to stay in that unforgiving, lonely place. She knew that place too well to want to move back there again, no matter how much she felt for Jed. She headed for the door. "Okay," she said, "I'll leave you alone. But if you decide you want to come back in, I guess you know where to find me."

"I guess I do." Jed raised one hand in a half wave. His eyes stayed glued to the desktop.

Laurel pushed through the door to the main office and walked down the hallway as fast as she could. She walked and kept walking. She walked out the main entrance, across the parking lot, and along Redwood Avenue toward home. She stepped over the scraps of crepe paper and wire, the ones that were too small for the clean-up crew to sweep away. She felt a tear run down her cheek, but she didn't turn back.

CHAPTER 21

"Laurel, have you got enough popcorn bowls?"

Laurel jumped up off the rug and joined her father in the kitchen. "There are only four of us, Dad."

"I just want to be sure."

"We're okay, Dad. Honest."

She looked back at the other girls, and all of them smiled nervously. They were in Laurel's living room around a coffee table made from an old tree trunk. Laurel and her father hovered over the stove across the breakfast bar, shaking the saucepan across the burner. The pop-pops went from tiny pings to sharp taps, like a kid pounding a roll of caps with a hammer. The apartment smelled like buttery toast.

Micki and Bets sat on the new sofa with the Indian rug over the back, while Page sat across from them on the floor. Laurel trotted in and out of the kitchen, carting bowls of popcorn and checking on her dad. As if her father knew that these two pairs of girls didn't quite know how to talk to one another, he leaned over the counter and said, "I saw the end of your parade today. I thought your float was terrific."

"Thanks," Micki replied, a little embarrassed. This was a lot more awkward than she'd thought it would be when Laurel asked them over here in the heat of the parade excitement. This apartment was so different from Micki's big tract house; or Bets's, where cows came up to the windows and mooed. Laurel's place was brand new and spare. It was obvious that only two people lived here. And Laurel's dad, who looked young and wore sandals and blue jeans, made such a big deal about having them. It felt as if Laurel had never brought any friends home before.

"Do you want to hear some music?" Mr. Griffith asked, skirting out from behind the breakfast bar and kneeling next to the stereo. The speakers were set on concrete blocks and all the records were stored in fruit crates.

"Sure," Micki said, "as long as it doesn't sound anything like the Flintstones."

"The what?"

"Never mind."

They all laughed. Micki wondered if it was weird for Laurel to have her father hover like this, but Laurel didn't seem to mind. Her dad said that he used to be a teacher in San Jose, so maybe he was used to hanging around with teenagers.

Mr. Griffith put a record on that sounded like some kind of New Age flute, then stood up and clapped his hands together. "Well, I'll get out of here and leave you girls alone. I've got work to do." He grabbed a spiral notebook off the breakfast bar and trotted upstairs.

"Thanks, Mr. Griffith," Micki called.

"Thank you," Bets echoed.

After he left, Micki found herself wishing that he might come back again. The four of them sat there, crunching their popcorn, licking butter off their fingers, and still not knowing what to say.

"What's your dad working on?" Micki asked, feeling like she was at one of her parents' awful cocktail parties.

"He's going back to school. To the university," Laurel answered.

"Oh," Micki said, trying to imagine having a father who was a college student.

They sat some more; Bets lightly kicking the tree-trunk table with her boot, and Laurel sort of humming with the record.

Page broke the silence this time. She looked right at Micki, and said, "I never thanked you for repainting my locker, Micki. At first I thought it was Laurel. But . . . thanks."

Micki swallowed, feeling almost like she was gagging on a little piece of popcorn. Even though they'd gotten past the locker incident, it was still not something she wanted to talk about. "How did you know it was me?"

"I saw the red paint on your jeans."

Micki was suddenly aware that everybody was staring at her. "So," she said, changing the subject in her best take-charge voice, "what should we do with the Haunted House now that we won the float contest? I'm in charge of that, too, since I headed the float committee, so if you have any great ideas, let me know and maybe I can put them through."

Page and Laurel looked at one another.

"Maybe we should make it a freshman lunchroom," Bets said, smiling at Micki.

The others thought about it for a moment, then shook their heads. The school administration would never approve.

They thought some more. "What do you think, Page?" Micki finally asked.

Page rested her chin in her hands. Her cheeks were still purply pink from the cave-girl rouge she'd worn for the parade. "What about an art gallery," she said suddenly, looking at Laurel. "For the whole school."

Laurel's eyes welled up and she took off her glasses, pretending to clean them on her sleeve.

"What do you think of that idea?" Micki asked Laurel.

"I think it's great," Bets answered instead.

"Sure," Laurel managed. "It sounds great."

There was a nod of agreement and a definite ease of tension in the air. Now when they looked at one another, at least they could smile.

"So is anybody going to the dance tonight?" Micki asked.

Bets shook her head.

"I don't think so," said Laurel.

"No way," said Page. She looked at Micki. "How about you?"

"I think I've had enough of guys for one week."

"I know," Page agreed. "Jason Sandy is a royal creep."

Suddenly they were all talking at once.

"Tell me about it."

"Boys," scoffed Bets, "you never know whether they're going to act normal or well . . . well, like cavemen."

"Or if they're even going to talk to you," Laurel said, in the saddest voice of all. She stared off, suddenly looking as spacy as her father's music.

Page waved a hand in front of her face. "Laurel . . . are you okay?"

Laurel relaxed and playfully batted Page's hand away. "I don't care what you say, I agree with Bets. Guys are weird. You never know what they're going to do. I think we should all stay home from this dance tonight."

Micki raised her Coke can. "Okay. I say we stay away from the game, too. I say we have an antihomecoming. Just the four of us? What do you think?"

They looked from face to face, not sure that they wanted to spend a whole evening together; not sure they were really meant ever to be friends. But no one wanted to turn down Micki's generous offer.

Page lifted her soda can, too. "To us. To staying home and talking about what a brilliant job we did today!"

230

"To us!"

"To the freshmen!"

All four of them took big swigs of Coke, then giggled when the soda fizzed up their noses and dribbled down their chins. Then they looked at each other again and tried to smile at the beginning of this strange, new friendship.

CLASS of '89

SOPHOMORE

Micki looked across the table at the telephone shelf again. Past the fruit basket and the pepper mill and the *Sunset* magazine. She saw them as clearly as she saw the telephone and her mom's calendar. Car keys.

Micki swallowed hard. Her parents had taken her dad's Audi. The Saab was in the garage. She could try it. If she left right at the end of the game, she'd beat her parents back. Sure it would be terrifying to drive alone. Sure it was a very long way. If she got caught, her parents would ground her until graduation. If she got pulled over by a policeman, she'd probably wouldn't get a driver's license for the rest of her life.

Micki scooped up the keys and headed out the back door to the garage. She inserted the key, threw her things in the backseat. She pushed the button to the electric garage door opener and the back of the garage slowly began to come open, the neighborhood yawning through it, beckoning her out into the streets. She turned the key in the ignition.

Micki signaled at the bottom of the hill and turned onto Redwood Boulevard. More rain. More splatter. The windshield wipers whipped back and forth at a hyped-up pace — about the speed of Micki's heart. She was gearing up to face the freeway. Getting on was the hardest part, she told herself. After that she could stay in the same lane all the way down to Sacramento. She grasped the steering wheel more tightly.

Just then a car pulled out in front of her. It was so close and so unexpected that Micki thought it was a dream for a moment. It was a big golden Mercedes, and it rocked when the driver saw Micki and slammed on the brakes. Micki had to swerve. She did it as hard as she could and hit the brakes even harder. She felt the car skid, the brakes lock. For a horrible five seconds it seemed like nothing she was doing would slow down the car, and it was turning in a full circle. Then there was a rubbing sound of shrubbery against the side door, the wheels going bump, thump, off the road, and a sudden tilt that threw Micki against her seat belt. When it was over the car was at a dead stop, but it was also halfway down a drainage ditch at the side of the road.

Micki got out and stood at the side of the car. It was really raining now. Pouring. Micki stared at the car. She stared at the rain and the street and the traffic whooshing by. Then she put her face in her hands and began to sob.